What the critics are saying…

4.5 *unicorns* "*WindWorld: Rapture's Etesian* is set in a war-torn world that envelops you and draws you into the lives of the characters… *Charlotte Boyett-Compo* has created a unique world that I thoroughly enjoyed visiting. The trials that Kynthia and Leksi encounter and conquer are exciting and laced with strong emotion. I highly recommend the journey that you take with this wonderful story." ~ *Enchanted in Romance*

4 *unicorns* "I loved the fact that the main character in this story is a fighter, a warrior woman… *Ms. Boyette-Compo* has a way of twisting a plot so that you do not know what is going to happen until the very end. I enjoyed this book tremendously." ~ *Enchanted in Romance, Another View*

4.5 *Stars* "*Charlotte Boyett-Compo's* style of writing has always been compelling and intense. *Rapture's Etesian* is no exception… This is a wonderful story where in a world filled with tragedy, two people meet and bond and build a deep true relationship. Kynthia and Leki will stay with me for some time as I thoroughly enjoyed reading their story. I look forward to more reading pleasure from the capable pen of *Charlotte Boyett-Compo*." ~ *Ecataromance Reviews*

4.5 "This book is certainly different from any shape-shifter story I have read. Kynthia is a woman in control and intends to keep it that way. Leksi is used to being in control, but finds the one woman he can let down his guard with. Together this couple is dynamite and the love scenes are explosive. *Charlotte Boyett-Compo* has done a wonderful job of combining two characters both with very strong wills and makes them submit to each other in a way that makes them stronger." ~ *The Romance Studio*

"In *Rapture's Etesian, Charlotte Boyett-Compo* has continued the saga of the Reaper. The reader will get a chance to become enchanted with Kynthia who is something rather unique. She is the only female Reaper. ...*Rapture's Etesian* to any lover of the Reapers, paranormal or of dark romance. This book is definitely a keeper on this reviewer's bookshelf." ~ *Love Romance Reviews*

4 cups "*Rapture's Etesian* is a book that will keep you reading until the very end. It's a great adventure of shape-shifters, vampires, kings, queens, and evil versus good. If you like erotic paranormals, this book is for you." ~ *Coffeetime Romance Reviews*

Rapture's Etesian

Charlotte Boyett-Compo

ELLORA'S CAVE
ROMANTICA PUBLISHING

An Ellora's Cave Romantica Publication

www.ellorascave.com

Rapture's Etesian

ISBN # 1419952811
ALL RIGHTS RESERVED.
Rapture's Etesian Copyright© 2005 Charlotte Boyett-Compo
Edited by Mary Moran
Cover art by Syneca

Electronic book Publication April 2005
Trade paperback Publication October 2005

Excerpt from *Longing's Levant*
Copyright © Charlotte Boyett-Compo

Warning:

The following material contains graphic sexual content meant for mature readers. *Rapture's Etesian* has been rated *E-rotic* by a minimum of three independent reviewers.

Ellora's Cave Publishing offers three levels of Romantica™ reading entertainment: S (S-ensuous), E (E-rotic), and X (X-treme).

S-*ensuous* love scenes are explicit and leave nothing to the imagination.

E-*rotic* love scenes are explicit, leave nothing to the imagination, and are high in volume per the overall word count. In addition, some E-rated titles might contain fantasy material that some readers find objectionable, such as bondage, submission, same sex encounters, forced seductions, etc. E-rated titles are the most graphic titles we carry; it is common, for instance, for an author to use words such as "fucking", "cock", "pussy", etc., within their work of literature.

X-*treme* titles differ from E-rated titles only in plot premise and storyline execution. Unlike E-rated titles, stories designated with the letter X tend to contain controversial subject matter not for the faint of heart.

Also by Charlotte Boyett-Compo

Desire's Sirocco
Ellora's Cavemen: Legendary Tails I anthology
Longing's Levant

About the Author

Charlee is the author of over thirty books, the first of which are the WindLegend Saga that began with WINDKEEPER. Married 39 years to her high school sweetheart, Tom, she is the mother of two grown sons, Pete and Mike, and the proud grandmother of Preston Alexander and Victoria Ashley. She is the willing houseslave to five demanding felines who are holding her hostage in her home and only allowing her to leave in order to purchase food for them. A native of Sarasota, Florida, she grew up in Colquitt and Albany, Georgia and now lives in the Midwest.

Charlotte welcomes mail from readers. You can write to her c/o Ellora's Cave Publishing at 1056 Home Avenue, Akron OH 44310-3502.

Rapture's Etesian

Chapter One

Leksi Helios was their prisoner and completely at the mercy of his captors. Though he was sore—his cock raw from the friction of their cunts sliding roughly down his rigid length—he would not let them know he was hurting. He would not allow them to see his humiliation, could not allow the bitches to know how helpless he felt. Keeping his teeth clenched, his eyes locked on the ceiling, his hands balled into tight fists, the only sound he made was the occasional grunt as thighs gripped his own and shapely asses rocked against his pelvis. The singular emotion showing on his handsome face was the brutal stamp of fury hardening his amber gaze.

"Pretend all you like, warrior," the red-haired one cooed. "But we know you are enjoying this."

"By the time we are finished with you, you will know your place." It was the blonde who spoke and her blue eyes held unmistakable vengeance.

"Does it matter if he enjoys it or not, Sisters?" the tall beauty with the coal black hair inquired with a chuckle. "I have come twice on his staff and intend to come a few more times ere the night is flown."

"Again, Celandina?" the oldest of the women asked. "Do you want to wear his cock to the nub?"

Lying atop the brawny warrior, Celandina's hands were under his taut ass, her long fingernails pressing viciously into the flesh. Her teeth latched on his pap. She suckled the pebbly flesh, running her tongue roughly over the tip, then released the hardened nub and turned to look up at her aunt.

"He'll last a long time with a sweet cock like this," Celandina replied, raising and lowering her body like a piston. "I am enjoying this whether he is or not!"

"Well, you've had enough of him, Sister. Time to share," the flame-haired woman complained.

"Aye, I have only ridden him once. My cunt is itching to have his cock thrust up inside it again," the youngest of them—a petite brown-haired waif with conical breasts—said with a sigh.

"Wait your turn, Haidee," vermillion-haired Ophelia insisted.

Celandina's lush lips pressed into a mock pout, but she pushed up from the slick body beneath her and rolled to her back as her sister, Ophelia, climbed atop the bound warrior.

"Captain Leksi Helios," Celandina sighed as she turned to her side and ran her fingertips along the tight jaw of their prisoner. "Such a potent name for a potent man."

"He has yet to spurt," the blonde complained. "How do we know he is potent?"

"I will make him spurt, Erinyes," Ophelia stated. "Just watch." Grinding her lower body on the hard length of their captive, she bent forward and swung her lush breasts against the warrior's chest, the rubbing causing her nipples to harden.

"Perhaps he does not like women," Erinyes said with a snort. She ran her fingers through the thick curls of her blonde hair and lifted the heavy length to cool her fevered body.

"Is that it, warrior?" Ophelia asked as she brought her face close to his. "Are you the pleasure hole for some hulking general? Do you like your balls squeezed by rougher hands than ours?"

Leksi shifted his narrowed eyes to the amused green gaze of the woman raping him. A muscle leapt in his cheek but he kept his mouth shut. Even when she threw back her head and laughed at him, he refused to voice the rage that was striving to break free.

"I do not see him spurting, Ophelia," Erinyes taunted in a hateful tone.

"He may not be spurting but he's leaking like a sieve," Ophelia chuckled. She ran a hand between their bodies. "Or is that me?"

The laughter of the women so infuriated Leksi that when the redheaded slut smeared their combined juices across his tight lips, he could no longer keep quiet.

"You fucking bitch!" he howled, jerking against the chains that secured him wrist and ankle to the bed. "Unchain me and I will show you what rape truly is!"

Celandina clucked her tongue as she thrust her hand through his thick brown hair and anchored his head. "Watch that pretty mouth of yours, warrior, lest we remove your tongue."

"*Unchain me!*" Leksi bellowed.

The hand in his hair tightened, gripping his dark curls in a savage twist as his head was jerked toward the beauty with the ebon tresses.

"Not until you are well-broken to saddle, little man," Celandina hissed. Gone was the amusement in her glistening black eyes. Her lovely face was set in lines of authority. "You are ours to do with as we please."

"For as long as we please," Ophelia put in.

Helpless, unable to free himself, splayed open to the ravishing of the four women who had jammed their shapely bodies upon him over and over again for an hour now, the warrior squeezed his eyes shut and thrust an explosive hiss through his clenched teeth.

"He can't hold that erection much longer," Galatea, the women's aunt remarked. She was standing off to one side, observing. As yet, she had laid no hand to their captive. "The tenerse lasts only so long, my sweets."

Leksi could still taste the cherry-flavored brew they had forced down his throat. The sickeningly sweet liquid had claimed him faster than any fermented drink of which he had ever partaken but instead of intoxicating him, it had stiffened his cock to a steely shaft that throbbed with unwanted desire. Under normal circumstances, he might well have been amused by the rigid erection, but it had become painful and his frustration was mounting.

"The Amazeens swear by it," Ophelia commented. "I can see why they use it on their enslaved menfolk."

"Aye, but we do not want to make him bleed. He'll be of no use to us come 'morrow if you overuse him this eve," Galatea advised. "With any luck, Kynthia will want to try his measure before we sell him to our sisters from Lemnos."

At hearing his fate was to be sold to the Amazeens, Leksi roared. He cursed the women so viciously, struggled so violently, Ophelia was unseated and flipped off him, landing heavily on one well-padded hip.

"*I will see you roasting in Hell for this, you diseased sluts!*" Leksi shouted.

Galatea cocked a slim white brow as the warrior bucked and twisted against his bonds. The flesh on his wrists was bleeding, as was the skin on his ankles. His broad chest was heaving as he continued to call them every filthy name ever created for women. Sweat glistened on his handsome face. The rise of his rigid shaft repeatedly jabbed the air as he thrust his hips from side-to-side.

"He has a very colorful vocabulary, doesn't he?" Ophelia queried.

The women—four of them naked as the day they were born and the other clad demurely in a soft white gown of flimsy gauze—sat watching their captive straining and cursing until at last he stopped, exhausted from his efforts. When he was still, his harsh rasping of breath the only sound of which he was capable, they were amazed that the stiffness of his cock still held.

"Remarkable," Galatea noted.

"Should we...?"

"Leave him be," Galatea recommended. "When the pain gets too much for him, he will ask one of us to drain his staff."

"Never," Leksi whispered, his eyes closed so he did not have to see the women.

"We will see, warrior," Galatea told him.

Long into the night, the throbbing member between his legs plagued Leksi Helios. There was no lessening of the rigidity, no surcease from the excruciating ache that caused sweat to cover his body. His senses had become so heightened that he fancied he could smell the musk between the legs of his tormentors. He fancied he could taste their starchy juices on his dry tongue, feel the pebbly surface of their vaginal linings.

"When you are ready," the older woman said softly. "We will relieve you of the torment warrior. All you need do is ask."

"No," he croaked, shaking his head weakly from side-to-side.

"You have to admire his willpower," Ophelia remarked to Erinyes.

"The only thing I admire about him is the size of his cock," Erinyes said with a snort.

He thought he lost consciousness for a few moments. The pain had become all encompassing and he was in such torment, he was ashamed to feel tears easing down his cheeks.

"Just ask, warrior," Ophelia recommended.

"No."

Galatea sighed heavily. "Stubborn man," she said, shaking her head.

"Let him suffer," Erinyes scoffed. "I enjoy watching him being tortured."

Another hour passed in silence. The room had grown chill as the wind from the nearby sea stole through the window. Draping themselves in their gowns, the women sat upon plush chairs pulled close to the bed upon which Leksi lay. They commented that despite the coolness that had enveloped the room, the warrior was sweating profusely though his flesh was ridged with goose bumps.

"The cold has not caused his staff to shrink," Ophelia said, pulling a shawl around her shoulders.

"Nay, but it has shriveled his balls," Erinyes observed.

"Not so. 'Tis the tenerse that has caused that," Galatea informed them. She studied the juncture between his muscular thighs, admiring his manhood despite her lack of interest in being serviced by it. "All the concentration of his seed is waiting to be released from those precious jewels."

Watching the cords standing out in the warrior's neck, the women's aunt grew concerned. His face bore a dull carmine shade as he strove to endure the discomfort in his cock. Moisture crept from the corners of his tightly closed eyes and his heels dug into the softness of the pallet. Galatea was worried the man's heart might burst.

"Go to bed, children," the older woman commanded. "It will be a while yet before Kynthia arrives, if she does."

"But—" Celandina started to protest, but her aunt held up a hand.

"Do as I say."

Grumbling amongst themselves, the women knew better than to argue with their aunt. The old woman was well into her fifth decade of life and wise far beyond her years. Her orders were never to be disobeyed. Reluctantly, the four sisters left, even Erinyes, each casting a whimsical look upon their prisoner.

Leksi felt the old woman's eyes on him and he opened his own, turning his head a little so he could see her where she sat upon the tall, throne-like chair beside the hearth. The two of them were alone and all was still save the low moan of the wind beyond his prison's walls.

"Why me?" he asked, his voice hoarse.

Galatea shrugged as she settled herself more comfortably in the chair. Her bare toes were stretched out to the warmth of the flames and she wiggled them to relieve the ache of advancing age. "You were handy," she replied.

"I was riding along, minding my own business," the warrior complained. "For once, I wasn't looking for trouble."

"Aye and such an enticing sight you made upon that big roan brute," Galatea said then sighed as she thought of the warrior sitting so tall and straight in the saddle. She smiled. "A more befitting mount for you would have been a Rysalian black, perhaps."

"Aye, well, a Rysalian would cost me two months' salary," Leksi snapped.

"But such a beast could easily have outdistanced us. That little roan of yours was barely any competition for our horses."

"And that damned arrow you shot me with was no competition, either!" he threw at her.

Galatea glanced at the scratch that marred his left forearm. "Haidee needs to work on her aim. She was going for your thigh."

"I'm lucky I didn't break my neck when I fell," the warrior stated.

"You didn't feel a thing once the initial sting pierced your flesh," the older woman admonished. "Like a drunken sailor, you tumbled off your horse and landed limp as a wet blanket on the sand—unconscious and unable to cause us any trouble." She giggled. "Until the girls began mounting you!"

Her words drove deep into the warrior's libido, and Leksi swallowed hard for the agony between his thighs made him want to sob with frustration.

"All you need do is ask and I will relieve you," Galatea said gently.

"I've had enough cunts abrading me this eve!" he snarled.

Galatea cocked her head to one side. "There are other ways I can relieve you, sweet one." She held up her hand, palm toward him then slowly closed her fingers until she had formed a loose fist. Slowly she raised and lowered her fist.

"You bitches like to torment men, don't you?" he grated.

"I am a widow," Galatea said in a conversational tone as she leaned her head along the back of the chair. "His name was Ocnus but he was anything but incompetent between the covers." She sighed. "He was a very good teacher."

"What did you do? Screw him to death?"

Galatea laughed, and lowered her head to look at him. "You are a marvel, warrior. Do you know that? Not only handsome but quick of wit."

"Lucky me," Leksi grumbled.

"We are all widows," Galatea continued. "Well, all save Kynthia who has never married and Haidee."

"And each of you murdered your menfolk or else sold them into slavery to the Amazeens," he accused.

Galatea drew in a long breath then exhaled slowly. Pushing up from the chair, she came to sit on the bed beside him. Her eyes roamed over his heavily muscled chest. She put a hand on the sculpted ridges of his abdomen.

"Please, don't," he pleaded with her, ashamed of his weakness but the torment was now almost more than he could bear.

"Ocnus died at the battle of Nebul, the capitol of Pleiades. For that reason alone I despise the Pleiadesian king," the older woman continued. "My beloved was killed along with his brothers Iorgas and Jirkar. Killed as well were the husbands of my nieces Erinyes and Celadina. It has made them both a bit mean, Erinyes more than her sister."

"If you mean the blonde and the black-haired one, they are more than a bit mean," Leksi disagreed.

As though she had not heard the warrior's remark, Galatea traced the puckered crease of an old wound on her prisoner's side. "Haidee was too young to have a man at that time but

Ophelia was engaged to a wonderful boy named Phaon. He, too, fell beneath the savage blades of the Nebullian horde. Still one more reason to hate all things Pleiadesian."

"Many Venturian warriors fell during that battle," Leksi told her. "My oldest brother and my father were among the slain."

Galatea looked up at him. The sweat poured from his face and his lower lip was bloody from where he had bitten it to keep quiet. "Were you there?" she asked.

He managed a quick nod then grunted as he felt his staff jerk at the older woman's nearness.

She circled the scar on his side. "Is that where you received this?"

"A love tap from a Nebullian whore who tried to run me through," he answered.

"Ah, yes," Galatea drawled, and her gaze grew hard as flint. "Their women warriors are particularly cruel, I hear."

"No crueler than the five of you," Leksi muttered.

Glancing out the window where the night shadows had gathered in the courtyard, Galatea studied the darkness for a moment. "She might not come home tonight," she said as though to herself. "Oft times, she camps out in the mountains, preferring the solitude of the soft winds and the trickling streams to her kinswomen."

Leksi was not listening to the woman. He was suffering so greatly, he could not imagine red-hot pinchers and thumbscrews causing more pain. Tears slid slowly down his cheeks and he gave in to a sob that shamed him but was as unstoppable as the wind skirling through the palm fronds.

Turning her attention back to the warrior, she listened a moment to his harsh panting then calmly reached out to wrap her fingers around his straining staff.

"Oh, by the gods, lady, don't!" Leksi begged.

"Ocnus reveled in the feel of my hand circling his cock," she whispered.

"Please!"

"When I was still a virgin and he made the trek from Nauplius to my home in Geryon, we would steal off to the banks of the Celeus and lie there for hours on end. He would touch me — most honorably, I swear to you — but he taught me how to touch him to the best advantage."

Aware of the gentle up and down motion as the older woman's fingers slid softly along his cock, Leksi held his breath. The feeling was one of sheer pleasure and he ceased to wriggle about on the bed.

"He meant for me to go to our wedding bed with my maidenhead intact," she continued as she increased the pressure on his turgid staff. "But that did not mean that he did not reciprocate as the months passed and our Joining day grew closer."

His vital juices were seeping from the slit of his penis and made the friction of her hand upon his flesh even more enjoyable. He caught a whiff of his own muskiness and began to tremble.

"He had such strong hands," Galatea remembered. "His fingers were long and tapered and could delve into spots that caused me to squirm like a speared fish on a branch." She ran her thumb into the warrior's slit and spread the sensitive lips.

"Ahhh..." Leksi moaned, and felt no shame at lifting his hips up from the damp mattress.

"The first time he slipped one of those glorious fingers inside me, I thought it was his cock for I had my back to him," she said then laughed. "He nipped my neck and reminded me I was his virgin and I would remain so until he would seat himself fully within me."

The sexual talk was enflaming Leksi's body to such a degree he felt he would combust if his rod did not explode. He was quivering from head to toe, his legs shaking as he dug his heels into the mattress.

Galatea slipped off the bed and stood beside it though her tight hand was still wrapped around the warrior's cock. "Oh, the wondrousness of his touch as he manipulated my clitoris!" she breathed. "I had never known such exquisite pleasure. When I came, it startled me at first, but then I felt the rapture of that itch subside to a very pleasant memory that I wished more than anything to repeat."

She leaned over him and slipped her tongue into the slit of his cock.

Leksi Helios was not a novice to the art of lovemaking. He had known more than his share of women and broken many to saddle, but never had he experienced such a wild stab of desire grip him as he did as the older woman's mouth replaced her hand upon his staff.

The pressure was a sweet agony that drew upon his flesh in such a way he could have stayed that way forever. His climax was a suckle or two away now, but he wished nothing more than to prolong it for the sensation was enveloping his entire world.

Galatea was pleasantly surprised at the taste of him for his essence was not particularly salty nor was it of a foul consistency. She knew from her years with Ocnus that a man's seed often tasted of the last food of which he had partaken and taking that flavor into one's mouth was not always enjoyable. This warrior's juice was thick but it bore a bit of sweetness.

Her lips were drawing from him every last bit of strength, and his limbs felt boneless even though they strained against the building ardor within him. As her tongue slid down his rigid length and lapped hungrily at his balls, he groaned so loudly, he was surprised at the sound.

Chuckling deep in her throat, Galatea slid a finger beneath his ass and up into that puckered little hole even as her lips claimed his staff in a tight, deep suction that took her lips to the very root of his member to press hard against the wiry curls. She wiggled her finger, pressed her thumb hard against the indention of his male pleasure spot between the anal opening and his balls, and then felt the burst of his cum shoot like a cannonball coursing down the back of her throat. The jerk of his flesh within her mouth nearly gagged her but she swallowed quickly, her tongue pressing hard against the underside of his rod.

"God!" Leksi shouted.

The orgasm was more intense than any he'd ever experienced in his thirty-six years—and he'd had more than his share. It felt as though his climax would go on forever. When at last he was depleted, he sagged limply on the mattress, drained of energy as well as his life juice. Though he was aware the older woman still sucked gently upon his root, he was beyond reaction, past a lingering quiver of his muscles.

Galatea withdrew her lips and hands from his flesh and straightened up. She sat down beside him once more and placed a warm hand on his belly. "Think you can sleep now, warrior?" she asked. "The one we brought you here for will be arriving soon, I hope. Are you anxious to see her?"

Leksi Helios was so used up he couldn't even grunt an answer to her. His eyes fluttered closed and within a matter of moments, he was sound asleep, his head tilted to one side.

It had been many years since she had performed such an intimate act, for she had never thought to again. In her three decades of marriage to Ocnus, not once had her hands or limbs, or tongue encircled another man. Since his death, she had slept alone, no male of her acquaintance worthy enough to share the bed Ocnus had made for them by hand. Her enjoyment of the sexual union had been laid to rest alongside her beloved husband.

"Sleep well, warrior," she whispered, and kissed her fingertips before placing them lightly on the Venturian's slack mouth.

Getting up, she looked about her until she spied a coverlet thrown across a chair. She fetched the light wool and spread it gently over the naked warrior's muscular body. Lifting the coverlet, she took one last look at the large staff that now lay sleeping against the warrior's thigh. A tender smile tugged at Galatea's mouth then she lowered the coverlet. Going to her own bed, she stretched out across the mattress as the wind sang in the palm fronds beyond her room.

Chapter Two

Kynthia was bone-tired as she slipped into the common room of her aunt's villa. All was dark, the inside servants already in their beds. Only the sentries at the gates had been awake to welcome her but she had refused the offer of a footman to light her way to the villa's portico. She preferred doing things for herself.

The common room smelled of the mixed perfumes worn by her four sisters and it was not an unpleasant aroma that greeted her. Scant illumination shown from the dying embers in the hearth but there was enough sky-glow coming through the windows to light her way through the silent halls.

Trudging wearily up the long, curving stairs, the young woman stopped in mid-step and thought of going back downstairs to fetch a cool goblet of wine, but she was too dog-tired after a day of hunting in the high mountains beyond the villa. The goblet of wine would be heavenly but a warm bath and a clean, fresh set of sheets was more enticing. Gripping the banister more firmly, she pulled herself up the chairs, her footsteps slow.

Perhaps it was the sensation of a stranger present in the villa or a light snore that caught Kynthia's attention as she moved past one of the guest rooms. Most likely, it was the opened door to a room kept closed off that halted her steps and drew her toward the darkened doorway. No candlelight glinted on the bedside table but then again none was needed for an errant beam of moonlight fell unerringly upon the bed and the man lying upon it.

Kynthia pursed her lips for she knew exactly why the man was there. Padding quietly to the bed so she would not wake him, the young woman paused at the foot and stared at the lengths of chains securing bare feet to the foot posts. Lifting her eyes to the headboard, she made out the glint of chain there, as well. Spread-eagled upon the mattress was a male who was—she knew without a shred of doubt—as naked as the day he had popped out of his mother's womb.

"Damn it, Aunt Galatea!" Kynthia growled beneath her breath.

For more years than she cared to remember, her aunt and sisters had been trying to saddle her with a mate. For just as many years, she had balked at the notion and refused to give in to their silly antics. If it wasn't a man they'd purchased from the vicious Amazeens, it was a traveler they'd waylaid along the road and dragged home in chains, drugged out of what feeble mind he had to begin with and completely used before being foisted off on her.

This one was by far the handsomest offering to date, but despite his obvious male beauty and excellence of body, Kynthia wasn't in the least bit interested. Dark, curly hair, long eyelashes and perfectly chiseled features might entice women like her sisters, but they did nothing for Kynthia save annoy her.

Shaking her head at the ridiculousness of her aunt's continual ploy to shackle her with a man, Kynthia turned away, the naked man on the bed already out of mind until the raspy voice stopped her.

"Woman?"

Rolling her eyes, bracing herself for either the hateful sting of the prisoner's spleen or the uselessness of him pleading to be set free, Kynthia turned to find the warrior staring at her. "What?" she snapped.

"Water?" he whispered.

Knowing her sisters had used the man brutally, a tug of compassion touched Kynthia's tight jaw, relaxing the clenched muscle. She looked to the bedside table but there was no water carafe sitting there. It was just like her sisters to abuse the ignorant prick then deny him even the most simple of creature comforts. Erinyes was known to starve a man for days on end until he did her bidding without complaint. How long this one had been held Kynthia could not know for she'd not been home for two weeks and had been expected three days earlier.

"How long have you been here?" she queried.

"A day," he answered weakly. "Longer. I don't know."

His accent intrigued her for she knew a Venturian when she heard one though she had never spoken to one of that country's warriors. A light brogue—not unpleasant to the ears—slurred his words as much as his apparent weakness slowed it. His voice was deep, the inflection of his words bespeaking of a higher class of citizen.

"I am thirsty. Water?" he asked again.

Letting out an annoyed breath, Kynthia left the room and tramped down the stairs. It didn't matter if her footsteps woke the entire household. Truth be told, she was up to verbally—if not physically—sparring with one or more of her sisters. After pouring a goblet of water for the stranger, she went to the cupboard in the dining area and poured herself a generous libation of Chrystallusian brandy. Stomping back up the stairs— angry that no one had ventured forth to quiet her heavy footfalls—she flounced into the room and stood there with both goblets.

"Are you the one for whom they attacked me?" he asked, licking his lips as he stared at the goblet in her left hand.

"I knew it!" Kynthia snapped. "I need to have a long talk with my aunt!"

"You weren't a part of it?" he asked, trying to swallow. "You didn't ask them to kidnap me?"

"They had no permission from me, I can assure you!" she replied. She placed the brandy on the bedside table then bent over the prisoner, sliding her right hand under his head to lift it. She placed the goblet of water to his lips.

The ripe cherry smell of tenerse was heavy in the air as she leaned over him. She pressed her lips tightly together, for that was one drug she found almost as detestable as the deadly Maiden's Briar, used on the tips of the scimitars of Hasdu warriors.

"Did they drug you?" she asked, and straightened up a little as he pulled his mouth from the goblet to answer her.

"Shot me," he said, cocking his head to the left.

Kynthia looked down and saw the dark slash against the tan of his muscular arm. "Must have been Haidee," she commented. "She can't hit the side of a stable when she's standing right beside it!"

He licked his lips, his action pleading silently for more water so Kynthia gave it to him. When the goblet was drained, she eased his head back to the mattress and straightened.

"You are Kynthia?" he asked again.

"Aye, that I am."

"So what is wrong with you?"

"With me?" she gasped.

"You can't get your own man so they have to steal one for you?"

Kynthia lifted her head. "I don't want a damned man!"

"Oh, you're one of those and they are trying to break you of chasing skirts, eh?" Though his words were insulting, there was no fire in them.

"Why do all men think if a woman has no use for them she craves another woman?" Kynthia sneered.

"Because that is the way of it," he told her.

"No, it isn't!" she spat. "I have no use for a man because I don't care to be a slave to one! I can go and come when and where I please. I am not answerable to anyone other than my own conscience. I am not forced to clean for some sloppy man or cater to his slobbering needs. I don't have to wash or mend his clothes or get up at the break of day to cook his meals or stay up long after I should be sleeping so I can warm his bed! I don't have to endure his pawing or have him ramming into me whenever the whim strikes or feel his slimy cum running down my damned leg!"

"You're nothing like your sisters, huh?" he asked.

"Why aren't you erect? I'm surprised you're still not as stiff as a Chalean blade," she mumbled.

"I would be if your aunt had not taken pity on me," he said softly as he closed his eyes.

Kynthia blinked. "My aunt?" she questioned.

"The little woman with white hair," he answered.

Suspicion narrowed Kynthia's eyes. "What did she do?"

Despite the limited light cast from the moon glow through the windows, Kynthia saw the blush that stained the warrior's cheeks. He opened one eye to look up at her. "She's good at her craft," he replied. "Her Ocnus taught her well."

Kynthia's mouth dropped open and shock widened her pale gray eyes. "You lie!" she accused.

The warrior opened his other eye. "Why would I and for what purpose? I'm as good as dead anyway."

"We're not going to kill you, idiot. Come morning, they'll turn you over to the Amazeens since I don't want you and—"

"Aye," he snapped. "I'm as good as dead."

There were worse fates than being sold to the Amazeen, but most men didn't believe so. Apparently, this one felt being handed over to the women warriors was a death sentence. As well it might be, if he did not behave.

"She lay with you?" Kynthia wanted clarification.

"Which one?" he snorted.

"My aunt, fool!"

"No," was the reply in a voice that was stronger than before and filled with annoyance. "She sucked my cock." He smiled faintly. "And was damned good at it, I must admit."

Stunned to the very core of her soul, Kynthia staggered back. She was staring at the bound man as though he were a demon from the slime beneath the Abyss.

Leksi Helios studied the woman standing so rigidly at the foot of the bed upon which he was chained and wondered why she was so astonished by his statement. Surely, he was not the first male to be helped by this woman's aunt.

After a long moment of charged silence, young woman shuddered. "I want you out of this house now!" she hissed. "I'll take no chance on Galatea coming near *you* again!" She knew the key to the lock attached to the chain was on a cord draped over one of the foot posts. She snatched it off the foot post and made quick work of the shackle binding his left ankle.

Flexing his leg as his ankle was released, Leksi winced as the lock on his right ankle sprang loose for the woman's nails had scratched him in her haste.

"Interfering old crone," the woman was mumbling as she came around the side and unlocked his left wrist. "Meddlesome old witch!"

Leksi's arm was asleep and fell uselessly upon the mattress when the shackle popped open. The sting of pins and needles pricking him as blood returned to his limb and the aching pull of his shoulder having been flexed at an awkward angle when he tried to raise it, made him wince as he listened to the litany of insults being heaped upon this woman's aunt.

"Nosy old hag!" Kynthia swore. "Why the hell can't she leave me alone? She knows I have no use for a rutting male!" She opened the lock on the warrior's right wrist then stood there glaring down at him. "Get the hell up and out of my sight! Do you hear me?"

Leksi's limbs were all but useless as he tried to push himself erect. The coverlet was hindering his legs and his arms so weak he could not throw aside the obstruction.

"Oh, for the love of Alluvia!" Kynthia cursed. She reached down, snagged the coverlet, and dragged it off him.

The cool wash of air dragged over Leksi and he shivered. It mattered little that the woman was staring unabashedly at his nakedness. What was one more set of eyes on his manhood this night? What bothered him most was the uselessness of his arms and legs as he tried to rise.

"Where are your damned clothes?" the woman demanded.

"How the hell would I know? I didn't strip myself!" he threw back at her as he managed to swing one leg off the side of the bed. His bare toes touched cold marble and he groaned.

Kynthia made a hissing sound that sounded more serpentine than human as she spun around and began searching the room for his clothing. Spying a pile of something lying in the corner, she went to it and grabbed it. The feel of leather and coarse wool assured her these were men's clothes. Without looking at them, she flung them toward the bed but something heavy fell to the floor at her feet and she bent down to scoop it up.

"I did nothing to you or those sisters of yours," Leksi grumbled as he snatched the leather britches from the bed.

Staring down at the object in her hand, Kynthia's forehead puckered in a confused frown.

"I was on my way to Qabala though only the gods know what I thought I could accomplish there," the warrior was saying as he clumsily thrust his legs into the britches. "If I had known five rampaging female rapists were out looking for a victim, I would have kept my ass in Tasjorn!"

The crest was of finely worked silver and lay heavily in her hand as she walked to the window to see the thing beneath the bright moonlight.

"At first," he said, as he pulled the loose tunic over his head and yanked it down with no care to whether the material tore or not. "I thought it was a band of Hasdu riding down on me but no!" The last word was drawn out in mockery. "Not Hasdu but rutting women looking for a man to ravage!"

Kynthia lifted her eyes from the medallion in her hand to stare at the man who was jamming his arms into the sleeves of his uniform tunic. She flinched and stepped back as he came to his feet and swung a wide leather belt around his lean waist. She almost reached for him as he staggered, but he grabbed the headboard to steady himself.

"Raping, ravaging and pillaging, horny women!" he added. He had no idea where his boots were and didn't care. He was being given a chance to flee this house of madness and even if the soles of his feet were cut to ribbons, he did not care. Without a glance at the woman huddled at the window, he exited the room in a near run. The slap of his bare feet on the stairs seemed overly loud.

"Are you allowing him to leave?" Galatea asked as she came into the room. She yawned and scratched at the silk covering her flat belly.

"Do you know who he is?" Kynthia whispered her eyes as wide as saucers.

"A man I thought would make you a good mate," Galatea replied. "I guess I was wrong about this one, too."

"Leksi Helios!" Kynthia hissed. "The Captain of the Venturian Guard!"

"I think Celadina said as much," her aunt responded.

"The Captain of the Venturian Guard!" Kynthia repeated. "A High Warrior!" She rushed to her aunt and shoved the medallion at her. "Konan Krull's right-hand man!"

Galatea glanced down at the silver medallion. "Aye. So?"

"What if he brings the guard to our doorstep, Aunt?" Kynthia whispered. "What if he has us arrested?"

Amusement lit the dark brown eyes of Galatea Atredides. "Think you he will want his men to know what we did to him, Kynni?" she asked. "Do you honestly believe he will go about advertising the fact that he was run to ground by five women, abducted and repeatedly raped?"

Kynthia groaned and dropped to the floor, covering her face with her hands as she rocked back and forth. "Leksi Helios," she whimpered. "He is the third most important man in the Venturian capitol at Lyria!"

"And a man who could have been your mate if you had but tossed the dice in the game, my niece," Galatea reminded her.

As fearful as she was that the man who had slammed out of that room would bring the might of the Venturian Guard down around their ears, Kynthia was infuriated at her aunt's single-minded purpose. "*I do not want a mate!*" she yelled at the top of her voice. "*And you know why!*"

"How would you know until you have one?" Celadina asked from the doorway. Behind her, were the rest of Kynthia's sisters. "Not all men are like the one from Basaraba, Kynni."

"And you were going to sell him to the Amazeen!" Kynthia grated.

"Well, we were going to try, but I imagine once they found out who he was, they'd have declined the deal," Ophelia supplied. "We would have been forced to let him go." She grinned. "Although I wish we could have kept that cock of his!"

"Oh, I bet the Amazeen would have bought him. If not them, then the Hell Hags would have. The witches would have bought him just to parade him naked before their Tribunals. He would have brought a clutch of gold sovereigns," Erinyes grumbled.

"I disagree," Haidee said. "I don't think either the Amazeen or the Daughters of the Night would want to take a chance of having Lord Konan Krull come after them."

"Oh, what do you know?" Erinyes scoffed.

"You had better hope he is too ashamed to report this to the Venturian High Council," Kynthia told them. "We've already made a bad enemy of this man and if…" She slapped a hand to her mouth. "The sentries!"

Galatea shrugged. "I left word they were to let him pass unchallenged if he came riding out on his own." She yawned again then turned to go back to her bedroom. "I figured you'd be stupid enough to let that prime specimen go."

Ophelia went to the window and looked out. She chuckled. "I hate to tell you this but he's taking your horse, Kynni."

The women rushed to the window in time to see the warrior racing from the stables. When he glanced back over his shoulder and saw them, he gave them a one-finger salute that brought a gasp to Erinyes' lips and a hoot of laughter to Galatea.

"I like that man," the older woman giggled. "He's got balls of steel dangling on him."

"That's my horse!" Kynthia groaned. "That's my baby!"

"Well," Galatea said with a shrug. "Go after him and get your baby back." She slapped her niece on the shoulder and walked off.

"That's my horse," Kynthia whined.

"Did you see what he did?" Erinyes snapped.

Celadina nodded. "Aye, but I'd have done the same." She wrapped her arm around her sister. "Let it go, Eri. We've seen the last of him."

Her sisters gone, Kynthia stood in the center of the room, the badge of Leksi Helios' office lying in her palm, and bemoaned the theft of her beloved Rysalian stallion. She'd raised the beast since birth and he was like the child she'd never have.

"He stole my horse," she said. "The bastard stole my horse!"

"Then get him back!" her aunt yelled before slamming shut the door to her bedroom.

Looking down at the medallion in her hand, Kynthia closed her fingers over the cool metal. "Aye," she said, gripping the badge until the edges pressed painfully into her fingers and the heel of her hand. "You'd better believe I'll get my baby back!"

Chapter Three

Leksi flew past the sentries, expecting them to try to stop him, but other than a curious look, they ignored his passing. He craned his neck around to make sure no arrow or quarrel was aimed at his back but the sentries were huddled around their fire, cups in their hands. Their negligence added further fuel to the anger invading the warrior's gut, but at least one good thing had come of that wicked night—the stallion beneath him.

The beast upon which he was straddled was as fleet as the wind rushing through Leksi's hair. Sleek muscles bunched and stretched as the large gray stallion raced through the night. His gait was even, his willingness to allow a strange rider upon his back a relief. Even without the benefit of a saddle, the beast gave a very comfortable ride. A blanket would have been better than only the broad bare back, but Leksi had not wanted to waste time in finding one.

"A Rysalian stallion," Leksi said to himself as the horse churned up the miles separating them from the Mad Rapists, as the warrior had labeled them. Perhaps not adequate compensation for all he had suffered at the women's hands but a prize he had no intention of returning, even if a man—or woman's—horse was oft their most valued possession.

The stallion was a rare prize, indeed. Without doubt from superior stock, well-trained, well cared for, the beast was a veritable gift from the Prophet this ill-fated night.

"And he belonged to you, didn't he, Kynthia?" he yelled aloud. "Well, he's mine now, bitch!"

He would never forget the names of any of the women, but two he would brand into his memory like battle scars—Celadina, who had been the first to savage him and Kynthia, who had not even considered him worthy of an Amazeen's purse.

A frown hovered over Leksi's face.

"Why didn't you think me worthy?" he wondered.

To be cast aside by a woman did not set well with the Venturian warrior. He'd never been turned down before. The insult grew worse with every mile over which the magnificent beast sped. By the time he cleared the gate at Tasjorn, the capital of the Ventura Province, his anger was a sharp prod that pricked not only his ego but his heart as well.

* * * * *

Kratos watched his friend as Leksi pushed his food around on the plate—piling it first to one side then scraping it across to the other to mound it there before returning it to its starting point only to begin the process again.

Leaning back in his chair, the older warrior folded his arms and studied the man who—though much younger—was Kratos' superior. Strangely quiet for over a week now, hardly any appetite to speak of, a dark, and the brooding gleam in his eye were all signs Leksi Helios had something on his mind. It was only a matter of time before the Captain of the Venturian Guard scraped up the courage to broach the matter with his old friend.

Leksi glanced up, looked down, and then glanced up again. Kratos was staring at him. "What?" he asked.

Kratos raised a bushy brow but remained silent.

Giving up on the fare that had grown tasteless over the past few days, Leksi dropped his fork and wiped his mouth on his napkin although no food had passed his lips during the evening meal. He swiped up his tankard of mead and finished off what was left. He looked at Kratos as he put down the tankard. "I've a question for you, Kratos," he said.

Kratos nodded but did not reply.

"How do you...?" Leksi began then stopped to clear his throat. He tried again. "How do you know when a woman is bothering you?"

A second bushy brow shot up then lowered to a mystified slash across the deeply lined forehead of the sixty-year-old Viragonian warrior. "You have a woman bothering you, boy?" he asked in his gruff voice.

Leksi threw out a negligent hand. "Maybe," he replied.

"Define bothering."

Leksi blushed. "You know — annoying the hell out of me."

"Have you asked her to cease?"

The blush deepened. "I've not seen her in several days, but that hasn't stopped thoughts of her from plaguing me!"

Kratos said nothing for a moment then reached up to scratch his weathered cheek. The rasp of his fingers against a beard already thick despite a close morning shave sounded like sandpaper against wood.

"Well, it's been a long time since thoughts of a woman have plagued me but let me see if I can remember," Kratos answered at last.

Leksi leaned forward. His respect for Kratos Hesar rivaled only that he bore for Konan Krull, the Lord High Commander of the Venturian Forces.

"You think about her all the time," Kratos stated. "Can't get her out of your mind." He waited as Leksi nodded then told him to go on.

"You can't eat," the older warrior said, and looked down at the food on his friend's plate. He ran a gnarled sword hand through his thick crop of short salt and pepper hair. "You don't sleep all that well if at all."

Leksi frowned. "Aye, hardly at all." He motioned the tavern maid to bring them each another tankard of mead, but Kratos waved off the offer of another for himself.

"Where was I?" Kratos asked. "Oh, yes. Everywhere you look, you see her face."

"Aye," the younger warrior said in a miserable tone of voice. "In the water, in the clouds, even in the damned mirages floating over the sands!"

"She pretty?"

"Glorious," Leksi replied. He slumped in his chair. "With eyes the color of molten steel and hair like freshly minted silver."

"Silver?" Kratos challenged, his head snapping back at though he'd been struck. "How old is this woman, boy?"

"Truthfully, I don't know," Leksi answered. "Twenty-four or so."

"And already her hair is gray?"

Leksi shook his head. "Not gray, Kratos, but silver — a rich, gleaming shade unlike any I've ever seen. Unbound, I'd wager it would touch her hips."

Kratos frowned. "I've heard of women who have had something tragic happen to them and their hair turned white, but silver?"

"I have a notion something evil might well have happened to her," Leksi agreed. "And that evil was most likely perpetrated by some shithead man."

"Um. Go on. Describe her for me."

"She's not too tall but tall enough." He held a hand level with his chin. "Up to here, I'd say. Slender with delicate hands." He smiled. "And the cutest little toes a man could suck on all day." He ducked his head. "Or so I would imagine. I didn't see them but her boots were small."

Kratos' face crinkled with amusement. "Is that so?"

Leksi continued without looking up. "She has high cheekbones, long eyelashes, a mouth the color of plump, ripe cherries." His face turned dreamy. "A long, swan-like neck, creamy shoulders and a small waist I wager I could span with both hands." He put his hands together to illustrate the size. "Broad hips well-suited for birthing many strong sons and pretty daughters."

"Really?" the older man encouraged, his lips twitching.

"Aye, and long, shapely legs made to wrap around a man's neck and…" Leksi stopped, his face flaming as crimson as the cherry lips he had just described.

"And is this paragon of beauty as bothered by you as you are by her?" Kratos inquired.

Leksi's shoulders slumped. "Aye, well, that's just it. She isn't."

"Leading you on, is she? Swishing her ass at you, smiling coyly then flitting away."

"Not exactly."

"Rubbing up against you as she passes? *Accidentally* touching you so you'll respond by touching back?"

"No," Leksi sighed. "I've never so much as laid a hand to her."

"Is she already taken, then?"

"I don't think so." He shook his head. "No, I know not. She says she doesn't want a man."

The tavern maid brought a fresh tankard to their table and apologized for the delay, citing the crush of patrons for the evening. When she left them, Kratos asked his companion if the silver-haired woman was even aware of his existence.

"Aye, but she wants nothing to do with me," Leksi answered.

"Not enamored of your sweet little body, eh?" Kratos chuckled. When his friend looked up and shot him a warning look, the older man held up a hand. "What is this lovely one's name?"

"Kynthia," Leksi muttered.

Kratos' brows shot upward again. "Well, well, well," Kratos stated in a singsong voice. "So it is to be a pale moon to your blazing sun. I find that interesting. The gods are up to their old tricks, huh?"

Leksi thought about it a moment. "Her name means pale moon?" At Kratos' nod, he sighed. "Aye, well she has the color of the moon with those eyes and that wondrous hair."

"So where did you meet this lovely lady?"

Leksi glanced away. "About."

"About," Kratos stated. "Were you introduced to her?"

"Not exactly," Leksi said. "Her aunt took me to meet her."

"Perhaps you could speak with her family then, and—"

"*No, hell I can't!*" Leksi shouted, drawing the attention of the others in the tavern. He lowered his voice though his tone was sharp and insistent. "I cannot!"

"You want me to?"

Leksi snorted. "Only if you don't mind winding up being sold to the Amazeen," he replied.

Kratos stared at him. "Don't tell me you've become besotted by one of those vicious bitches!"

"No, no, no!" Leksi said, once more waving his hand in dismissal.

"She lives near the Amazeen, then?"

Leksi looked down. "Not far from their lands," he replied.

"Close enough for the Amazeen to be a concern, eh?"

"Aye."

The two men were silent for a few moments then Kratos scratched his beard again. "Well, you could always woo her."

Leksi looked up. "Woo her?"

Kratos rolled his eyes. "It means to court her, boy."

"I know what it means!" Leksi held out a palm toward his friend. "Woo her how?"

"Do you wish to woo her?"

Leksi groaned. "Aye, Kratos. I wish to woo her. I would like this woman as my life-mate. But how do I do this?"

"You woo her with flowers and sweets," Kratos replied. "A pretty bauble or two for her neck or arm."

Leksi snorted. "She's not a flowers and sweets kind of woman and I saw no adornment on her save…" He winced.

"Save?" Kratos encouraged, sitting forward.

"A leather gauntlet," Leksi answered in a low voice.

Kratos settled back in his chair, his mouth open. "She's a warrioress?" he asked after a moment of stunned silence.

"Aye, I believe she is. There was a crossbow and a quiver of quarrels beside her saddle and her horse was a Rysalian stallion well-suited for a High Warrior than a mere woman."

Speculation turned Kratos' dark brown eyes almost black. "Was? Are you telling me the stallion you now ride belonged to her?" Kratos asked with a growl.

"Well, aye. The beast was hers," Leksi admitted with a wince.

"You stole it from her, didn't you?" Kratos accused.

"I escaped on it," Leksi replied.

"Oh, this gets better and better," Kratos snapped. "Escaped? When? From where? From who?"

Leksi buried his head in his hands. "Just tell me how to keep from being bothered by her, old man," he said. "I can think of nothing else! I can't keep thinking about her if I can't have her. It will drive me crazy!"

"Well, you can start by returning her horse," Kratos told him. "To steal a warrior's horse—female warrior or not—is not a good thing. I thought you found that beast." He lowered his voice. "You told me you did! Leksi Helios, you lied to me!"

"I did find him…" Leksi defended himself. "…when I was fleeing her aunt's villa."

"Fleeing her…?" The older warrior held up a hand. "Return the beast and then we'll talk," Kratos ordered. He pushed his chair back and got to his feet. "I taught you better than to steal horses."

"I didn't know where mine was!" Leksi snapped. "He wasn't in the damned stable and I didn't have time to—"

"Return the woman's horse then we'll talk!" Tossing the price of his meal upon the plank table, the older warrior turned on his heel and exited the tavern, slamming the door shut behind him.

"Interfering old bastard," Leksi complained. "Meddling old prick."

"He'd make a good companion to my aunt, wouldn't he?" whispered a silky voice right behind him.

Leksi felt the point of the dagger pressing between his shoulder blades. He could also smell the scent of gardenia that had stayed with him long after he had fled the room where Kynthia had found him.

"Get up and let's walk outside, warrior," she said. "Make one false move, sound the first syllable of alarm and I'll run this blade through your black heart."

"How long were you listening to my conversation, wench?" Leksi growled, feeling the heat invading his cheeks.

"Long enough to hear that I bother you," she said, and he could hear the amusement in her voice. "And that you would like to woo me."

Gritting his teeth in humiliation, he told her he needed to push his chair back in order to rise.

"I am as quick as an asp, warrior," she warned. "No sudden moves." She removed the blade from his flesh.

Leksi eased the chair back and stood. He glanced down at the table to see if Kratos had paid for his meal, and upon seeing the warrior hadn't, told her he needed to reach into his pocket for his purse.

"Slowly," she agreed.

He fished into his pocket, took out the purse and counted out the change. Slowly, he placed the coins on the table and returned the purse to his pocket.

She placed her hand to the center of his back and stepped to his side so he could move away from the table. The tip of the dagger was now pressed to his rib cage but no one could see it for the hilt was hidden in the folds of her voluminous robe.

They walked out of the tavern at a leisurely pace, Leksi returning the greetings of many of his men. Few glanced at what they must have assumed was a slender lad walking beside their Captain. Those who did nodded knowingly for since Leksi Helios had no woman, they suspected his tastes might run elsewhere.

"Your men think you are a pleasure hole," Kynthia commented as he preceded her out the tavern door.

"They do not!" Leksi denied almost turning around to confront her but the light jab of her dagger against his rib cage warned him not to do so.

"Doesn't matter," Kynthia snorted. "Where is Aeolus?"

"Who?"

"My damned horse, fool!" Kynthia snapped.

Leksi had walked to the tavern from the barracks where he had been for most of the afternoon. The stallion was safely stabled within the grounds of the keep. In order to get there, they would need to pass the sentries at the gates of the palace as well as the guards who presided over the mounts of the higher-ranking warriors. Destriers were a valuable asset to the Venturian Guard and the mounts of the High Warriors were closely protected.

"He is within the palace grounds," Leki told her with a touch of smugness. "Well-guarded as befits a prime beast like him."

"Shit!" she exploded.

"Did you think you could just saunter in here and pick him up?" Leksi asked, turning his head to look at her. Within the hood of her metal-gray wool robe, her facial features were little more than a blur in the darkness. He was intrigued to see how pale her flesh was.

"I want my horse!" she stated between clenched teeth. "The handsome one ordered you to return him to me!"

Leksi stiffened. "You think Kratos is handsome? You need your eyes checked, woman!"

"That one has the face of a wise and experienced man," she told him. "Not the insipid appearance of a pretty boy like you!" She pressed the tip of her dagger a little more firmly against his ribs until the point penetrated the wool material of his uniform tunic. "Go get my horse and bring him to me."

Leksi Helios had been promoted to a High Warrior soon after his thirtieth birth month. As such, he was an experienced, skilled and highly accomplished soldier whose kills in combat numbered in the hundreds. In hand-to-hand battles, the count was well over two dozen. He was a brave man with little care for his personal safety when in the throes of war. During peacetime, he trained just as intensely as during times of hostilities. He was deeply respected by his men, feared by his enemies and held in high esteem by both the High Commander of the Venturian Forces, as well as the king. No one questioned the bravery or the capability of Leksi Helios and only three people dared give him orders.

The woman at his side was most assuredly not one of those three. Once before she had dared to issue him an order, and he had obeyed it simply to escape the clutches of the Mad Rapists, but now, there was no reason to do so.

Kynthia intuited the warrior's move before he made it, but so quick was his action she had no time to counter it. One moment she was holding a dangerous blade to her enemy's side and the next, her arm was stinging from the vicious hit that knocked the blade from her grip. Before she could retaliate, she was wrapped so tightly in a bear hug she could barely breathe. Her back to the warrior, her wrists clamped in a hand that felt like a steel band, she was lifted free of the ground and swung around so she dangled on his hip like a sack of salt. Arching her back, trying to kick her captor, she felt the bones in her wrists grate as he ground them together.

"Give me any trouble, wench, and I'll turn your shapely backside over my knee and wallop the hell out of you right here and now!" Leksi snapped.

Enraged beyond endurance, Kynthia let out a yowl of fury and bucked in his hold. In the doing, he dropped her to the ground and placed a hard boot in the center of her back, pushing in with enough pressure to cause her real pain, the heel of his boot bruising the area over her right kidney.

Leksi had no way of knowing the woman beneath his foot had suffered severe damage to her back many years earlier. The spot upon which his boot heel was pressing was causing her intense, excruciating agony that turned her into a quivering, sobbing mass.

"Warrior, no! Please don't!" she begged. "Let up! Let up!"

Stunned by the obvious pain in the woman's voice, Leksi jerked his foot from her back and dropped down beside her. He tried to gather her into his arms, but her howl of agony stayed his hand as she arched her back and flipped to her side, writhing on the ground like a dog crippled beneath the wheels of a carriage.

Then something happened that would forever haunt Leksi Helios. This brave, skillful warrior with nerves of steel and a head for quickly formulating the most complex of strategies became the unwitting observer of a scene so bizarre, so totally beyond his realm of understanding, he could do no more than hunker there—eyes wide, mouth open in silent denial, hands trembling as the very soul within his body quivered. The sights he was taking in would have unbalanced a lesser man for before his very eyes the beautiful woman at his feet was changing.

No longer did the pale flesh of her face intrigue him for it was now coarse and covered with layers of thick silver fur. The lovely gray eyes were blood red, glowing with chatoyant hues of green then white as light from the moon struck them. The lips like lush, sweet cherries were now leathery and skinned back from lethal-looking fangs. The pert, upturned nose had become an elongated snout with flaring, dripping nostrils. Delicate hands were being replaced with paws equipped with thick talons that scratched at the cobblestones as the woman tried to rise.

"My god," Leksi whispered, feeling his innards turning watery.

It was the sounds that stayed with him for the rest of his life, the least of which were the harsh rending sounds of fabric bursting its seams and material ripping apart. The resonance of joints becoming unhinged, bones cracking and sinews popping, flesh stretching like leather being pulled over the poles of a travois, organs making slurping noises as they rearranged themselves, squishing sounds as fangs—sharp and yellow as aged parchment—pushed from bleeding gums.

Kynthia Ancaeus arched her transformed back and stood there wobbling on four legs as she shook her large, lupine head from side-to-side. Staggering a bit, she sidled back from the human male staring at her. Her great bushy tail was low, curled beneath her belly, her pointed ears flat back against her head. Saliva dripped unchecked from her muzzle as she bared her teeth and growled low in her throat.

Understanding he was seeing something few men had ever witnessed and lived to tell of it, Leksi held out his hand. Within snapping distance of those dangerous jaws, he kept it there as he spoke.

"I did not mean to hurt you, little one," he said. "I was only trying to subdue you."

The growl was menacing and it meant business as the wolf moved closer to him.

"Forgive me," Leksi said, and his hand shook as he reached out to touch the wolf's head.

She snapped at him, the fangs clicking together and it was all the warrior could do not to snatch his hand back. He was breathing so quickly he felt lightheaded and his breath was harsh as he sucked it in through his nose, but he held his ground.

"Forgive me," he said again, and marveled that the wolf allowed him to touch her head.

The fur was coarse beneath his fingers and the bony protrusion of the head brought a feeling of sympathetic pain to his heart. This transition that had turned a human woman to a silver wolf must have hurt her tremendously.

She endured his touch though her low growl was a reminder that she had no trust for the male. As his hand smoothed over her fur and ran lightly over her shoulder, she wrinkled her nose with distaste but allowed it.

Leksi removed his hand and knelt there on his knees watching her. There was no doubt in his mind that should she wish to, this dangerous beastess could leap upon him and tear out his throat before he could utter a single cry. As she stood there in the rent remains of her gray wool robe, she looked every inch the predator.

"I will bring your horse to the stream that borders Ventura and your aunt's lands in the morning and—" he began but the wolf shook her head fiercely in denial.

Understanding fell upon Leksi Helios like a war banner over a fallen bearer—this was a creature of the night. Each time he had seen her it had been after the rise of the moon.

"At sunset tomorrow eve?" he corrected. "You promise you will meet with me?"

The great head bobbed up and down then the wolf turned and raced away so quickly, she was soon lost in the darkened shadows of the town courtyard.

Leksi knelt where he was until the howl of the wolf came from far away.

* * * * *

Kynthia huddled beneath the spreading branches of an olive tree. She was miserable and cold, her bones aching. Naked and defenseless, she kept watch on the hut behind which clothing hung on a clothesline. No one stirred so she crept closer to the slowly moving garments wafted on the evening breeze. Sniffing the air about her, searching for anything that might harm her, she approached the clothesline stealthily until she closed a hand upon a woman's gown and jerked it from its pins. Quickly, she turned and sprinted across the hillside, her upper body low, the garment clutched possessively to her bare breasts. Once she reached a spot she considered safe, she put on the gown, frowning at the rough feel of the peasant fabric as it touched her sensitive skin. Clothed, she continued on over the hills and down into the valley to her aunt's villa.

The sentries snapped to attention at the low whistle issuing from the darkness. The men recognized the lady's signal but were surprised when she came toward them, limping on bare feet. Though they offered assistance, they were rebuffed and stood scratching their heads as their employee's niece continued on to the villa.

"She hasn't been right since they brought her home from Uaigneas," Demodocus commented to his fellow sentry.

"Aye, well she ain't human no more," his companion whispered.

Her acute hearing took in the words of the sentries as Kynthia opened the courtyard gate. She limped up the marble steps to the portico then pushed open the door. Tired as she was, pain lingering to impede her movements, she knew she would never be able to climb the curving stairs. Instead, she headed for the pantry where darkness prevailed almost as completely as in the special room her aunt had built on the upper floor.

Like a very old woman—feeble and bent—Kynthia eased the pantry door closed and barred it from the inside. She supposed Erinyes would find fault with her choice of lodging for the coming day but there was nothing within the pantry that was of such vital importance it could not wait until sundown.

Upon sacks of flour and salt, Kynthia made her bed. Though uncomfortable and lumpy, it was better than the cold, bare floor. As she settled down, her thoughts were jumbled, mixed in with bitter memories that made her heart hurt.

It was the memory of the evil man who had changed her life forever that kept Kynthia awake through that long day. Even as she heard her sisters and aunt converse with the servants who had not been able to gain entrance to the pantry and had called the mistress for her advice, the young woman lay wide-eyed in the darkness.

Nor did she answer her aunt when the older woman called softly to her through the door.

"Minos," Kynthia whispered, loathing the name as much as she despised the one who had held it.

It had not been the vicious rape that had left a sixteen-year-old girl bruised and battered, broken and bleeding. The bastard's rough hands and chipped nails had gouged and pinched her flesh, his dirty fingers ramming into each orifice of her body as he used her. His foul breath and jagged teeth, filthy, unwashed body and sour odor had repelled her as he rutted over her. Though the painful invasion of his stumpy tool had hurt her soul more than her defenseless body, it had been his drunken assurance that she had enjoyed the defilement he had enacted upon her.

"You like that, huh, girl?" he had asked over and over again as he rammed his cock inside her torn vagina, flipping her over to invade another opening that brought screams of agony shrilling from her throat.

Finally flinging over to his back in exhaustion claimed by the potent wine he had been swilling all day, he ignored the girl he had deflowered so brutally. As he lay spent—his withered rod flopped upon his dirty thigh—she had crept to a rock, lifted it quietly then brought it down upon his ugly head, squashing the cranium like an over-ripe melon.

Over and over again, until there was nothing left but mush where once there had been brains and skull, Kynthia took her revenge on the man who had ruined her life. Staggering to her feet, she had begun the long trek to her parents' home in a state of icy calm.

"No man will want her now. She's damaged goods," her brother had warned their parents when the Healer had come and gone and Kynthia's wounds had been dressed.

"She's lucky the Tribunal does not sentence her to death for killing a man," her father moaned, burying his face in his hands. "What will we do with her now?"

"We must find her a good man," her mother had sobbed. "A gentle man who will overlook what was done."

"She murdered a man!" her father whispered. "Who will want to take her to wife knowing that?"

But one man had.

Even as the young girl lay healing, word came to her parents that a man wished her hand in Joining. With no expectations of anyone else ever asking for marriage to their deflowered daughter, Kynthia's parents had agreed. Despite screams of denial and pitiful cries of pleading, her father and brother had taken her to the island where her betrothed lived.

"I don't want you!" Kynthia had screamed at the man who had met them at the quay.

"Be quiet, girl!" her father had insisted. He would have continued but the man who would be his son-in-law had held up a hand.

"What is it you want, then?" the man had asked her.

There was no hesitation for Kynthia. "I want to be as strong as any man and just as heartless. I want to live my life as I see fit and never have anyone gainsay me!" Her hands had clenched into fists. "I want no man between my legs ever again!"

"Forgive her, milord!" her brother had cried out. "She has been unhinged by what happened."

A single glance from the man had silenced father and son. Extending a purse to them with a bride price that would equal any in the district, he bade them leave.

Hating every man who had ever drawn breath—her father and brother included—Kynthia did not care that her kin left her alone on the island with a man none of them knew anything about. If she had to, if it took a day, a week, a month or a year, she'd bash the man's brains out and flee the island. Never again would she be at the mercy of any man. Never again would any man ram his filthy rod into her.

"I have no desire for you in that way, wench," the man told her. "You need never lie with any man you do not wish to."

"Not even you?" she had sneered.

"Most especially not me," he had insisted.

"Then why did you buy me?" she snarled.

"To right the wrong, Sweeting," he said with a faint smile. "For my sister."

Chapter Four

Kratos sat bolt upright in the bed, his heart hammering as the door to his room was flung open. He would have flung himself to the left to take up his dagger but Leksi's voice stopped him.

"She is a wolf!" Leksi pronounced. He advanced into the room. Striking a light, he lit a lantern then shook out the thin piece of wood and tossed it to the table. "A beautiful gray wolf but a wolf just the same."

Having been rudely jerked out of a sound sleep, Kratos was understandably disoriented and a tad more than annoyed as evidenced by the large fart he let loose as he threw the covers aside. Standing in all his naked, brawny glory, the warrior's bodily note was loud and prolonged and carried with it an extremely unpleasant odor that caused Leksi to fan the air. "By the gods, Kratos! Have a care that you don't suffocate me!" he complained.

"Don't burst into my room whilst I am dreaming of having five dancing girls giving me the massage of my life then!" Kratos shot back. He scratched his balls as he padded heavily to the chamber pot then braced himself for a good piss. "What couldn't wait until I've put my head together, brat?"

"She's a wolf!" Leksi repeated. "Didn't you hear what I said?"

Kratos concentrated to make sure his aim was as sure as ever as he relieved himself. The old warrior prided himself in the fact that, unlike many men his age, he left no mess for the morning maid to clean. He glanced back over his shoulder, frowning. "Are you talking about the bothersome one?"

"Aye!" Leksi agreed. "She came to fetch her horse but things got a bit off track. I'll take the beast to her this evening."

Shaking his member, Kratos' frown deepened. "She's a changeling and you're going to meet her at eventide? How stupid is that, brat? Why not in the full light of day?"

"I don't think she's about in the daylight, Kratos," Leksi explained. He puffed out his chest. "I am not afraid of her."

"Well, you're not the brightest piece of material in the stack," Kratos reminded his young friend.

"Nor am I the dullest," Leksi returned. He plopped down on Kratos' bed, as the older warrior got dressed.

"I've heard tell of a gray wolf haunting the hills beyond," Kratos remarked. "Could be her."

"I hurt her," Leksi admitted, and when his friend turned to give him a narrowed look, the younger warrior blushed. "Not on purpose, though."

"And she is willing to meet with you?" Kratos inquired as he pulled on his uniform tunic. "Either the girl is curious about you or she's luring you to your death." He took up his belt and dragged it around his ample waist. "Perhaps I should accompany you."

Leksi shook his head. "She'll think it's an ambush. I'll go alone."

Kratos shrugged. "Suit yourself." He sat down to pull on his boots. "You will no matter what I advise."

As the two friends made their way to the barracks to break their fast with the other soldiers, Kratos kept a surreptitious eye on the young warrior and plotted a way to follow Leksi to the meeting place that night.

* * * * *

Kynthia woke long before the sun was high in the sky. The sacks of flour were soft enough but the salt and sugar had gone lumpy and poked her in myriad places to deny her rest. Staring through the almost-dark room, she listened to the servants going about their midmorning chores and listened in on their conversations concerning their menfolk. It was at such times she learned more about males than she had at the knee of her aunt, as Galatea instructed her on the ways of life.

As she had grown older, Kynthia had begun to feel an emptiness that at first merely annoyed her. She had tried to fill her waking moments with martial arts training, becoming the best horsewoman she could be, and learning strategy at the hands of the most knowledgeable warrioresses among the Amazeen. Despite grueling hours of training, the daylight hours were filled with loneliness and building restlessness. She was miserable most of the time and nothing she did seemed to alleviate the situation. The harder she worked, the more restless she became.

Kynthia did not understand what ailed her and sought out her aunt's counsel.

"It's not that your cycle is completely reversed from an ordinary woman's," her aunt had explained. "Training at night instead of during the day has its particular challenges but you will be the best night warrioress among all the tribes. As for the sleeplessness and discontent during the daylight hours, my guess is you are simply lonely, Kynni. You need a companion."

By companion, Kynthia knew her aunt meant of the male persuasion and such a thing was anathema to the young woman.

"I have no need of a man to burden me!" she exclaimed. "Besides, men sleep at night and war during the day!"

Well, men save the one who had purchased her from her father, and his was a different story...

* * * * *

"You want me for what?" Kynthia had shouted, backing away from the man who had bought her from her family.

"Now, wait before you jump to the wrong conclusion!" the man had asked.

"I might not want a man pawing me, but I sure as hell don't want a woman to, either!"

"That's not going to happen. Let me explain."

Despite mistrust of the man across from her, Kynthia snapped her mouth shut and surreptitiously looked for a weapon should he decide to attack her.

"There is a large rock just behind you, wench, but I warn you—before you could turn and reach for it, I would be on you like snow blanketing the highest alp."

Kynthia blinked. "You read minds?" she asked.

"I possess many talents and that is a minor one," he admitted.

"I will not be some woman's plaything," Kynthia stated. "Nor will I be someone's slave!"

The humor slipped slowly from the man's face. "We are all slaves to something, wench. At the moment, your master is righteous anger and he rides you more cruelly than any human owner could."

"What does she want of me?" Kynthia shouted. She did not care for word games and she sensed such activity with a man like this would be a losing endeavor.

"My sister was raped just as you were."

Kynthia sat down upon a large, flat rock. "She wants my help in slaying the man who attacked her?"

He shook his head. "No. He received his just punishment long ago and Callista, too, is long gone."

Suspicion narrowed Kynthia's eyes. "She is dead?"

"Aye, she is dead," he said.

Kynthia frowned. "I still don't see how—"

"My sister was considered to be the most beautiful girl child beneath the canopy of the heavens," he continued. "She had thick brown curls that swept the ground as she walked. Her eyes were the color of lush green foliage and she possessed skin sun-kissed with perfection. Suitors came from all over the world to vie for her hand."

"But that ceased when she was raped, eh?" Kynthia asked in a bitter tone.

His face became a mask of hatred. "She was a mere child when that Molossian bastard stole her from us. He used her like a common whore then cast her aside in search of his next victim."

"Molossian?" Kynthia repeated for it was a word she had never heard before.

"I would have gelded the son-of-a-bitch had I not been off-world at that time."

"Off what?"

"Never mind, just listen," he had snapped.

So she had paid attention to his tale, and when he was finished, she had stared at him. "Your sister must have been a very astute warrioress."

"What she knew, she learned from me and that by chance. On my world—"

"That's it," Kynthia grumbled, throwing up her hands. "I don't know what world you live in, milord, but apparently it isn't the one where the rest of us reside." She started to get up but he was so quick, she never saw him move until he was right beside her, his heavy hand on her shoulder. He kept her from rising and the strength in that one hand made it impossible for her to shake it off.

"You are right, Kynthia Ancaeus, I am not of your world. I am a Reaper. My name is Cainer Cree and I am from a place millions of miles from here called Ghaoithe. I have been here now for over seventy-five years and have not aged one day in all that time. I never get sick and if I accidentally cut myself, I heal in the blink of an eye. I have the strength of ten men along with the ability to read minds and…" He raised one thick dark brow. "If I could leave this island, I can fly."

Kynthia stared at him. Her expression left little doubt that she thought the man standing above her was a lunatic. She reached up to pry his fingers from her shoulder but she might as well have tried to pry a rock from cliff beyond.

"Callista took matters into her own hands and slit the throat of the bastard who brutalized her," Cree continued. "Instead of a dagger, you used a rock on Minos Daedalun. You had your revenge but that hasn't given you any satisfaction, has it?"

"Hell, no, it hasn't!" she threw at him. "If I could, I would go after every pervert I could find and rid the world of them! That would bring me great satisfaction!"

Cree shook his head. "No, Sweeting, it wouldn't, but it would go a long way in easing the pain you feel. Only finding your soul-mate will give you the true satisfaction you crave."

Kynthia struck at his hand with her fist but the hits had no effect on the man. He stood where he was and a smile tugged at the corners of his mouth. "I…don't…want…a…gods-be-damned…man!" she shouted.

"Perhaps not at this moment in time, but time has a way of moving on, Kynni, and loneliness is a terrible road to walk," he said quietly.

The softness of his words, the gentle look in his eyes brought the tears from Kynthia's eyes and she covered her face with her hands and sobbed violently, her shoulders shaking, her moans of grief pitiful to hear. She leaned into his hard chest when he hunkered down before her and pulled her into his brawny arms.

"Let it out, Sweeting," he whispered. "Let it all out and the wound will begin to heal."

Kynthia had shed no tears when Minos had savaged her. Nor had one teardrop fallen when she had begged and pleaded with her father not to bring her to the Isle of Uaigneas and sell her to the stranger who lived there. Now, the tears flowed like a river overflowing its banks and she clung to the man holding her as though he were a life raft.

"I know what it is like to be at the mercy of those who would rule your life, Kynni," he crooned to her. "I, too, know the frustration of not being in control of my own destiny, but I am offering you the means to live your life the way you see fit and be beholden to no one."

"N-no man will e-ever want m-me," she cried. "And I w-want n-no m-man!"

"Perhaps not at this moment in time," he repeated as he stroked the damp hair back from her forehead, "but you are young and beautiful and—"

She pulled back and looked up at him, her eyes red and puffy, and her nose running. "You think I am beautiful?" she asked.

He put his hands on her cheeks and stared into her swollen eyes. "You are as lovely as a spring morning," he replied.

When he released her, she ran the back of her hand under her nose. "Truly?"

"Truly."

For the first time, she really looked at Cainer Cree. So frightened had she been—and angry with her father and brother—she had paid no attention to the man who had bought her. Now, her face was only ten or so inches from his and she was staring into eyes the color of freshly drawn honey.

He was as handsome a man as any she had ever seen. Truth be told, his male beauty might well rival even the gods for he was tall with a flat belly and well-muscled arms. His hair was thick and curly, and as brown and as dark as a sparrow's wing. A soft, deep voice that commanded attention yet was very pleasant on the ear came from lips that were finely chiseled—pleasingly full, as her Aunt Galatea would say—and through teeth as white as the snow on the highest alpine mountain.

"You find me attractive, Kynthia?" he asked.

She nodded, her cheeks stained bright red, and tore her gaze from him.

"What would you say if I told you the man to whom you will one day give your heart would put my poor features to shame?" he inquired.

"Huh," Kynthia grunted. "You read the future, too, milord?"

"No, but someone who visited me not long ago can and she told me all about him."

Kynthia looked up. "Who is he? What is his name?"

Cree grinned. "Now, that wouldn't be fair, now, would it, if I told you?" When she started to protest, he held up his hand. "Besides, if I told you his name, you would seek him out and that is not what the Fates have in mind."

"The Fates don't always play fair either," she grated.

"They do what they feel is best for us, Kynthia."

"They wanted me to be raped by that bastard, Minos?" she challenged.

"No," he said, the smile slipping from his lips. "Sometimes evil slips into our lives. It is how we handle the adversity and sorrow that prompt the Fates to either reward or punish us."

"What was your evil's name?" she asked, sensing a tale in the sad depths of his golden eyes.

"Zenia," he replied. "But I will speak no more of that witch."

"Did you love or hate her?"

He scowled at her, and she caught a glimpse of the powerful man she understood he could be. "I despised her for she took me from the woman I loved. Ask me no more about that bitch for the mere thought of her drives me this close to Transition," he said, holding his thumb and index finger a hairsbreadth apart.

"Transition?" she asked with a sigh. "You speak in riddles, milord."

"You'll understand it all in good time, but for now, let's take a walk. There is something I would like to show you." He got to his feet and held his hand out to her.

Though she had vowed to hate every man who drew breath between then and Doomsday, she took his hand and allowed him to pull her to her feet. Once more, she marveled at the strength in his fingers and when he threaded his fingers through hers, she knew it would be senseless to try to pull free.

"I have no designs on you save to help you be the woman you want to be," he said as they started walking up a steady incline. His hut was off to one side and she asked him why the door was closed for it was a stifling hot day.

"I spend most of my time outside," he answered. "I find I no longer care to be cooped up."

They walked through a thick stand of trees with low-hanging branches until they came to what must have been the highest point on the island. Ahead and to her left, she could hear waves crashing and a soft, fine mist struck her face gently.

"I love the sea," she said, feeling the need to break the silence between them.

"I used to," he said. "And I still like to watch the tide coming in."

"You don't swim?" she asked.

A muscle ground in his lean jaw. "Not anymore."

It was to a tall cliff overlooking the ocean that he took her. The rocky prominence had a natural railing made of rock that rose up to waist height on Kynthia. When he released his grip on her hand, she strode forward and braced her hands on the top of the railing, and looked down.

Far below, the white-sand beach curled in a crescent shape around the base of the rugged cliff. Huge, jagged rocks were being assaulted by powerful waves and spray flew upward in a salty mist that looked almost like fog. Overhead, seagulls called to one another and rode the high currents, sailing past with graceful maneuvers that drew Cree's gaze.

"I miss that most of all," he said quietly.

Kynthia looked at him, remembering his boast that he could fly. "You weren't serious," she said, sensing a great sadness in the man beside her.

"Aye, I was very serious, Sweeting. Look there."

He pointed to an island just off the coast and Kynthia stared at the massive black bird that perched upon the spit of land.

"What is it?" she whispered, her words little more than puffs of breath.

"*The Levant*," he replied. "My ship."

Kynthia slowly turned her eyes to him. "Your ship?" she said, letting the words drop like heavy stones.

"My flying ship," he told her. "It is a machine from my world, from my time." His gaze grew wistful.

"Once I flew her to worlds far beyond my own. I soared higher than any eagle of this world has ever flown. In her, I had a freedom unlike anything you could ever imagine."

"What happened?" Kynthia asked.

Cainer was quiet for a moment. His gaze was dark and his wide shoulders slumped. He appeared to be weighing his words carefully before he spoke. When at last he did, his voice was low and devoid of emotion.

"On my world, a female who kills a male—no matter the reason—has no recourse under the law. She cannot plead self-defense if that was her motivation. She will not be afforded the use of a lawyer to argue her case. Her sentence will have been decided before she ever steps before the Tribunal and for her crime, her life is forfeit."

"That is a terrible system of justice," Kynthia commented.

Her companion snorted softly. "Justice? There is no Justice under Tribunal Law for a female. Her lot—be she peasant or princess—is that of chattel to be sold to the highest bidder. Depending upon her station in life, her value is the deciding factor in such matters."

"Your sister," Kynthia said. "She was executed?"

Cainer nodded. "While I was flying maneuvers near Oceania." He closed his eyes for a second or two and when he opened them, there was moisture rimming the golden orbs. "By the time I returned, she had been in her grave for nearly a week."

"Did no one tell you what was happening?" she asked, shock in her tone.

"My father would not allow me to be informed of Callista's fate." He smiled sadly. "She was my little sister and I loved her dearly. He knew I would have tried to save her if I had been told she was to be hanged."

Kynthia winced and put a hand to her throat. "And he couldn't save her?"

"He didn't want to," her companion answered. "To him, she was nothing more than a nuisance, a female to be auctioned off when the time came. Had she not killed the man who had raped her, she would not have received a decent bride price, for she was damaged goods."

"Like me," Kynthia mumbled.

"On Ghaoithe, such women are handed over to the brothels so in a way, it was best Callista met her fate at the executioner's hands. Had my father turned her over to such a place, I would have gone berserk and he knew it."

"But couldn't he have gone to your King and —"

"He *was* the King," Cainer stated.

"Oh."

"I came home to find my mother and father on holiday in the mountains. They had taken my younger brother with them. My older brother — the Prince Regent — stayed behind as token head of the State. It was he who told me about Callista."

"How did he feel about her death?"

Cainer shrugged. "No one loved her save me and…" He smiled sadly. "…and Aisling."

"Your sister?"

"Nay. The woman with whom I intended to Join." He turned and looked at her. "And the niece of the man who had raped my twelve-year-old sister."

Kynthia's eyes grew wide. "Twelve?" she echoed.

"A mere child," he repeated. "A babe, really, but old enough to procure a dagger and slip into Korsun Lalor's room and cut his throat from ear to ear."

"I am so sorry," she whispered.

"My only delight after that was in Aisling and the love we shared for one another. Not even my flying gave me the kind of joy it once did for whenever I left Ghaoithe, I could not help but remember what had happened when I had been gone. I worried that something would happen to Aisling."

"Did it?"

He shook his head. "No. I imagine she lived to be an old woman with dozens of grandchildren clamoring around her knee." He laughed. "She was a Shanachie, a storyteller who could spin yarns with the best of the bards. There would have been stories flying fast and furious from those pretty lips and her grandchildren would be sitting there mesmerized."

"Shanachie," Kynthia said. "What a beautiful word."

"She was a beautiful woman."

"You never Joined with her, then."

"No."

"Because of the woman whose name you don't wish to repeat?"

He nodded. "I learned that witch was going to harm Aisling, and I thought to lure her out into space and rid myself of her once and for all."

"I take it she was bothering you."

"Everywhere I went she showed up. Every event found her there in attendance. No matter where I turned, she was there. The very sight of her caused my stomach to churn. I loathed her and I feared what she might do if given the chance. I could not endanger Aisling's life so I climbed aboard *The Levant* and led that crone out to the very limits of our galaxy."

"You came here."

"Not by choice, I didn't," he replied. "Fate drew us here and when we landed, I wound up a prisoner on this island and she wound up dead at the hand of my warden."

"You are a prisoner here?"

He turned to look at her, fusing his gaze with hers. "Do you not know what this place is?" he asked. "Have you not heard the tales?"

"I know it is called the Isle of Uaigneas and I had heard a strange, wild man lived there, but beyond that, I don't recall hearing anything else."

"A strange, wild man," he repeated and grinned. "Aye, that describes me well enough."

Kynthia sniffed. "I don't find you strange and you have yet to jump up on the rock and bellow like a bull. Do you swing your arms, pound your chest and make grunting sounds like the apes on Ostara?"

"No, but once every third month I change into a wolf-like being and lope about the island in search of rabbits from which I drink enough blood to satisfy my ungodly hunger."

Pretending a huge yawn, Kynthia patted her mouth with her hand. "Oh, what a sight that must be."

"You'll soon find out," he said, the smile slipping from his face.

Kynthia started to laugh, but when she saw that he was watching her steadily, his face devoid of all humor she felt a tingle of unease quiver down her spine.

Chapter Five

Galatea glanced up as her niece came into the drawing room. She smiled and laid aside the sampler she was stitching. "You don't look as though you enjoyed your nap in the pantry."

"You know I didn't," Kynthia grumbled. She poured herself a goblet of her aunt's sherry and sat down before the roaring fire.

Settling back, Galatea braced her elbows on the arms of her chair, steepled her fingers and rested them under her chin. "Did you search out the handsome brute that made off with your horse?"

"Aye."

"And did you find him?"

"I found him."

"A veritable god, isn't he?"

Kynthia drained the sherry then threw the glass into the fireplace. As the goblet shattered, she turned her angry eyes to her aunt. "You took him against his will."

"We take them all against their will, Kynthia. Think you they would come here of their own accord?"

"Why did you do it?"

Galatea rolled her eyes. "You know we have been searching for a suitable mate for you and—"

"You took part in the attack against him!" Kynthia accused. "The others, you left for me to send on their way but this one you brutalized."

"Brutalized?" her aunt said, her eyes wide. "Nay, I did not brutalize that prime specimen. Taunted—perhaps. But brutalized?" She shook her head. "If he says so, he lies."

Kynthia narrowed her eyes. "You sucked his cock!"

A long sigh came from Galatea. "That I did, and what a big cock it was." She grinned. "Did you get a look at it?"

"No!" Kynthia lied.

Galatea raised an eyebrow.

"Well, aye, but I wasn't really looking *at* it!" her niece admitted.

"What were you looking at, then?"

"A very angry High Warrior!" Kynthia snapped. "And one who saw me change last eve."

The humor vanished instantly from Galatea's eyes and she sat straight up in the chair, her hands gripping the arms. "He saw you Transition?" At her niece's curt nod, the older woman flinched. "This is bad, Kynthia. This is very bad."

"I am to meet him tonight and get my horse back," Kynthia told her aunt.

"No!" Galatea denied. She came to her feet in a lithe bound that belied her years. "He'll have men there and they will try to kill you, Kynthia. You must not meet him!"

"I vowed I would, and I will keep that vow. He'll be alone."

"You don't know that!"

"Aye, but I do," Kynthia said.

"How?"

Her niece smiled nastily. "Because I bother him."

* * * * *

Leksi paced the ground from one tall date palm to another and started the trek again. The moon was high overhead, yet the lady for whom he waited had not appeared. He was growing concerned and his pacing increased. Now and again, he glanced over at her horse but the animal was standing placidly, ground-hobbled.

"Where's your lady, Aeolus?" the warrior asked. "Why isn't she here?"

The steed bobbed its head up and down, causing the bridle to tinkle. It pawed the ground a few times then lowered its elegant head to munch the oats scattered in front of it.

"Unconcerned about her, eh?" Leksi chuckled.

It was the pricking of the beast's ears that alerted the warrior to the fact he was no longer alone. Peering into the darkness, he saw a dark shape off to his left. The silhouette was about two and a half feet from ground to tip of a pointed ear. A passing moonbeam lit the silvery gleam of thick fur for a moment then traveled on into the darkness.

"I was beginning to worry, Little One," Leksi said.

The shape came no closer, but it turned its head and surveyed the surrounding area.

"I am alone."

"You were," said an amused voice.

Leksi spun around to find Kynthia standing right behind him. So quietly had she approached, his warrior ears had heard nothing. But his trained eyes flicked back to the animal he thought was the lady and found he was staring into a pair of inquisitive golden eyes.

"I call him Kirkor," Kynthia said.

"Vigilant," Leksi responded with the old meaning.

"Aye, for that he is."

"Your protector, milady?"

"At times. When I am in full Transition, I have joined his pack simply for the thrill of it. To run, to hunt, though I refrain from taking life. It is the challenge of the chase that I find exhilarating. Kirkor is the prime male of his pack and I believe he regards me as one of his own."

"As a mate?"

Kynthia shook her head. "He has a mate. I am simply one of the females to him."

Turning away from the warrior, Kynthia walked to her horse and reached up to stroke the bridge of its nose. "Did you miss me?"

The steed snorted and stretched out his neck to nuzzle his mistress.

"Was he good to you?" A nod of her mount's head brought a sigh of relief to Kynthia.

"Did you think I would abuse him?" Leksi asked.

"No, but not every male is as respectful of a beast as its owner is," she replied.

"Not every owner is as respectful of his beast as he should be," Leksi countered. "I was taught that it is a privilege to possess a stalwart mount and you treat one with consideration."

Kynthia looked over at the warrior and smiled. "That's a good thing to learn about you, Leksi Helios."

That smile brought a similar one to Leksi's lips, and he dug his hands into the pockets of his breeches. "Why Aeolus?" he asked.

"Because," Kynthia said, running her hand across the horse's neck and along its withers, "he is as fleet as the wind and just as strong. He has served me well on many a night."

"You only come out at night?" he asked.

"Aye, but I am not limited only to the evening. I just prefer it."

Digging the toe of his boot into the ground as a bashful boy would, the warrior lowered his head and spoke without looking at her.

"Are you not human, milady?"

Kynthia blinked. "Why would you ask such a thing?"

He glanced up at her. "You change," he said, and even in the moonlight, the blush stained his cheeks.

"Aye, I change, but I am just as human as you."

Leksi narrowed his eyes and his face took on a look of confusion. "But how is it possible that you become an animal? I thought only the gods and their ladies could do such things."

"I am a Reaper," she said. "And Reapers have abilities given to them from a man not of this world."

"A god."

"No, not a god, but as close to one as you or I will ever know, I suppose."

"Reaper," Leksi repeated. "What is it you harvest?"

Kynthia laughed, and the warrior looked up. The humor was evident on her lovely face and as she pushed a thick strand of silvery hair from her cheek, he sighed with longing.

"I harvest nothing save a cup or two of blood each day to keep me sane," she answered. "That is the price I pay for all the abilities I possess."

"What abilities?"

"Keen eyesight and hearing like my lupine counterparts, extraordinary strength and endurance. Healing capabilities far beyond the normal. The ability to live ten times longer than a normal person," she replied.

"I wouldn't mind having such abilities," he said.

Kynthia cocked her head to one side and studied him silently for a moment. "Even if it meant changing as I change?" she questioned.

"Perhaps."

"It is a very painful thing to Transition," she told him.

"Life is painful, milady."

"Not as painful as Transitioning," she scoffed.

He pulled his hands from his pockets and folded his arms over his chest. "Let me ask you a question."

She nodded.

"If I had possessed the powers you have when your aunt and her rapists attacked me, would I have been able to fend them off?"

"Easily," she responded.

"No matter that there were five of them?"

"No matter had there been ten of them."

He thought about that for a moment. "I believe I would like being a part-time wolf."

Kynthia snorted. "You think so now, but the reality of change is a bitter road to travel."

Leksi shrugged. "Would it mean having you to mate if I were to change?"

The smile slipped from Kynthia's face. "So you can use me whenever the mood struck?"

"So I could make love to you when we were both of a mind to do so?" he offered.

Kynthia came toe-to-toe with him. "Make love to or fuck?"

"Whichever you prefer," he answered honestly.

"I've been fucked," she spat, her eyes flashing. "The bastard raped me. He hurt me so badly I swore no man would ever touch me again!"

Leksi unfolded his arms and reached out a hand to touch her cheek, surprised when she did not flinch or pull away. Gently, he moved the pad of his thumb under her left eye, tracing the dark shadow that dwelt there.

"Give me his name and I will skin him alive," the warrior vowed.

Kynthia felt a funny little quiver in her belly at his touch, and his words drove straight to her heart.

"*One day,*" Cainer Cree had prophesied, "*you will meet a man whose hand will start a fire in your loins, milady. His gentlest touch will stoke that fire until it is a blazing inferno only his male potency can extinguish. When you find such a man, hold fast to him for you will know you have found your life-mate.*"

"Tell me who he is and he is as good as dead, milady."

Kynthia mentally shook herself. "No need," she said, her voice husky. "I killed the Basarabian bastard long ago."

The warrior put his other hand to her face. "I would slay a hundred dragons for you if you but asked."

"Dragons don't exist, Helios," she sneered.

"There are dragons, and then there are dragons," he said, gazing deeply into her eyes.

She made no move to stop him as he brought his face to hers and his lips touched her mouth in a soft, fleeting contact that made her heart race. When he drew back—his eyes locked on hers—she felt weak in the knees. Standing so close to him, she could see every little sun wrinkle and shaving nick on his face, and she reached up a finger to touch one spot where he had cut himself just that morning. The fresh scab came away on her finger and a single bead of blood bubbled to the surface. She caught it with her nail then brought it to her mouth.

Leksi groaned softly as his lady flicked out her tongue and tasted his blood. "I would never hurt you," he swore. "Nor would I ever allow anyone or anything to hurt you. I would cherish you as you deserve to be cherished and I would—"

He got no further for Kynthia threw her arms around him and jerked him to her, her lips closing over his in a hot, passionate possessiveness that made his head reel. His arms went about her waist and held her to him just as tightly. Her mouth was slanted across his, the tip of her tongue darting in and out between his teeth, dueling with his own tongue. Her fingernails were arched against his back and when he lowered his hands to her ass, she jumped, locking her legs around his hips, her ankles crossed behind him.

Leksi pulled his head back, his breath coming in a harsh pant. A throbbing erection was pressing intimately against her belly and when she wiggled against the feeling, he thought he would come.

"Easy, milady. Easy," he cautioned.

"I want to know what it is my aunt and sisters find so wondrous, warrior," she said. "I want to…"

He turned with her and walked to a soft, sandy spot where he dropped to his knees with a grunt. Leaning forward, he stretched out atop her, sliding down until his erection was thrusting insistently at the juncture of thighs.

"Feel me, wench," he said, grinding his hips against her. "Feel my cock aching to slide into you."

Kynthia shuddered and felt wetness between her legs.

Moving so he was lying along her thigh, he wedged a hand between them then thrust his fingers gently down the waistband of her breeches and found the slickness waiting at her crotch.

"Oh, my god!" Kynthia exclaimed. She arched her hips off the ground and in the doing partially impaled herself upon his questing finger. Digging her nails into his back, she drew in a breath and held it as he slipped his middle finger into her warmth.

She was tight and hot, and sweetly wet as the warrior moved his finger slowly and gently inside her. Though her nails painfully scored his flesh, he continued to stroke her, drawing from her little moaning sounds that made his shaft as hard as granite.

Whipping her head back and forth, Kynthia was lost in the pleasure invading her lower body. The sensations of heat and pulsing tremors made her nipples ache and she longed to have the warrior's lips suckling her.

"Suckle me," she heard herself say, and knew the blood had rushed to her face for she felt as though she had opened the door to a furnace.

Leaning over her, Leksi placed his mouth over the erect peak of one nipple straining the fabric of her blouse. The soft cotton was soon wet as he laved it with his tongue, swirling the tip around and around until he locked his lips over her nipple, stabbing at that sensitive nub with the tip of his tongue then drawing it into his mouth and between his teeth.

Kynthia was panting as though she had been running all out with Kirkor's pack. The pleasure the warrior was giving her was so intense, so powerful, she was quivering from head to toe. Her hips were off the ground, giving Leksi full possession of her nether region. When he pulled his mouth from her aching breasts, she moaned in frustration.

"Let me love you," he whispered. "Let me be inside you."

"Aye," she managed to acquiesce. She was beyond denying the warrior anything.

At her agreement, he was on his feet, ripping at his clothing as though it were on fire. He was staring down at her, she was staring up at him and when her tongue flicked out to dart across her upper lip, Leksi Helios freed himself from his breeches.

Kynthia's eyes went wide at the sight of that fully erect member. Thick and long, it appeared a weapon in her sight and she shrank back, fear turning her gray eyes dark. She crossed her arms over her breasts and—though she could not close her legs for he was standing between them—she drew into herself like a frightened child.

"No, milady," he whispered as he sank down in front of her. "Touch it and know it will not hurt you."

His hand closed over one of hers and he pulled it downward, feeling her strength and knowing if she had not been willing to allow him, he would not have been able to move that hand. When he closed her fingers around him, he had to steel himself not to shame himself.

Kynthia held that stiff cock in her hand and felt it throbbing in her palm. Her fingers barely met around the thickness of it. There was a soft heat that emanated from it to scorch her palm, and as he began moving her fingers up and down the length of his staff, she closed her eyes.

"It wants you, Sweeting," Leksi told her. "Feel how much it wants you."

She felt dominant with that mighty rod grasped in her hand. Were she of a mind, she could rip it off at the root, but her grasp turned soft as velvet as she stroked him.

Though he was still clothed in opened breeches and boots, he was as defenseless in her hands as a newborn babe and he knew it. She had hold of the very essence of him and Leksi was aware of her power. Her stroke was firm but gentle—not too tight and not too fast.

"You are very good at that," he managed to say.

"I listen well," she replied, thinking of the many times she had overheard her aunt and sisters discussing their conquests.

"Lucky for me, wench."

She smiled, but doubted he could see her for he was above her, blotting out the light of the pale moon. She looked up at his dark face, wishing she could see his expression but making a decision, she knew would affect them both forever.

"Undress me, warrior," she asked, her voice as soft as her touch upon his staff.

Though he wanted nothing more than to rip the clothing from her chest, Leksi leaned over and unhooked each button with infinite care. When the last one came undone, he put his fingers under the edge of the fabric and pushed it away from her breasts. Unbound, the soft globes fell sweetly into his palms.

Kynthia sucked in a breath as his thumbs moved back and forth over her turgid nipples, then circled them with the calloused pads.

"Please!" she whispered.

He lowered his hands down her rib cage, burning a pathway down her flesh until he lightly grasped her waist. She was trembling as his fingers found the closing of her breeches and opened them. Even as he drew the fabric down her legs, she had hooked the toe of one foot against the boot heel of the other foot and was pushing hard, grunting with the effort.

"I'll get them," he said, and moved back so he could grip the boots and pull them off.

Then he drew the breeches from her long legs and tossed them aside.

With her blouse pushed aside, Kynthia was lying exposed totally to him, her dewy flesh awash in the light of the overhead moon. A part of her reasoned that she should be ashamed of her brazenness, but the larger part of her was eager to know his thrust—his possession.

Leksi put his hand upon the dark patch of hair at her crotch and cupped her, allowing her to feel the heat of the heel of his palm against her clit. When she squirmed and lifted her hips, he pressed a bit harder.

"Lay still, wench, and let me pleasure you," he said in a gruff voice.

Kynthia stilled, though she lowered her hands to her sides and dug her fingers into the sand. She closed her eyes and concentrated on the delicious maneuverings going on between her legs.

The warrior slid his hand downward until he could bracket her nether lips with his index and ring fingers of his right hand. His middle finger moved down over his lady's clit then flicked upward gently, his fingernail making wicked contact with that sensitive little protrusion.

"Argh!" Kynthia cried out, and drew her lower lips between her teeth to help her keep quiet.

As he tenderly manipulated her clitoris with deft, possessive upward flicks of his nail, he watched Kynthia's face, smiling as he saw the strain on those lovely features and the light sheen of sweat that dotted her forehead.

"Concentrate, wench," he whispered.

Kynthia's eyes popped open for a moment, and then she squeezed them tightly shut. "What the hell do you think I'm doing, warrior?" she demanded.

Leksi chuckled to himself then dipped his middle finger into her oozing slit.

Kynthia squirmed as her lover-to-be slowly turned his finger around inside her. As his probe moved deeper into her, she could feel the knuckles of his hand pressing against her vaginal lips. When his finger crooked inside and touched some sensitive spot that made her entire body hum, she jerked her hips upward, wanting more of that sublime sensation.

"Kratos once told me to search for a small node that feels different than the rest of the lady's love walls," Leksi commented.

"I think you found it," Kynthia stuttered.

"Good," he said and withdrew his finger.

"No!" Kynthia gasped, her eyes wide.

"Do you trust me, wench?" he asked.

"I want you to…"

"Do you trust me?" he repeated.

"Aye!"

"Then get on your hands and knees."

"You'll not take me like that!" she swore, eyes flashing, teeth showing.

"No, I will not, but I wish to give you the ultimate in satisfaction and the way to do that is to have my hand inside you as you squat."

"Minos…"

"I am not Minos," he said firmly.

She stared at him for a moment, her body craving his touch, and when at last her lust could no longer be denied, she flipped to her side, pushed herself to her hands and knees, and shrugged out of her blouse.

"Lower your head and tilt your hips upward," he instructed, and she did as he commanded without a comment. As she moved into position, Leksi put his index and middle fingers into his mouth and wet them. Then with his palm downward, he gently slipped the fingers into Kynthia's vagina.

"Ah…" his lady moaned and wriggled her hip against him. "I like that."

"Then you should like this even more," he said as he probed the front wall of her vagina until once more he found the slightly raised area — about the size of a copper coin — and touched it.

"Aye," she sighed, the word drawn out with emotion. "I damned well like that more!"

Since he was kneeling beside her, Leksi reached under her with his free hand and laid his palm against her abdomen, just above the wiry curls, and pressed firmly upward.

"Oh, my god!" Kynthia cried out. She rotated her hips, tilted her lower body until the glorious spot Leksi stroked was in full contact with his strong fingers.

He could feel her body gearing up to come. As the walls of her cunt began to tighten, he slipped the hand pressing into her abdomen down to her clit and fingered it.

A sensation unlike anything she had ever experienced in her life shot over Kynthia Ancaeus. Her entire body quivered from head to toe and the heated gripping sensations pulsing within her lower body was awareness unto itself.

Leksi moved his fingers in and out of her in quick, shorter strokes and when her climax burst upon her, pressed those digits deep inside her and held them there, reveling in the quickening sensation that squeezed around them.

She was impaled on his hand, and gloried in the feeling. She could feel the fabric of his breeches rubbing against her bare thigh and even that sensation was wondrous.

Just as her aunt and sisters had predicted it would be.

When the last throb of her sex had ceased, her body felt limp and she collapsed upon the sand, dragging in deep, shallow breaths.

Leksi stretched out beside her, careful not to allow his stony erection to touch her. He pushed a damp strand of her hair from her cheek and bent over to kiss her shoulder. As he did, he saw the great, white male wolf staring back at him from ten feet away.

"Do you approve?" the warrior asked the wolf.

Both Kirkor and Kynthia agreed. She mumbled her concurrence and the wolf stretched out with his head between his paws and closed his eyes as though he was as tired as the human male.

"You did not hurt me," Kynthia said softly.

"It was not my intention to hurt you," Leksi responded, and cast the wolf a sardonic look. He doubted Kirkor would have allowed him to hurt the lady.

"But you did not gain pleasure from the mating," she said, opening her eyes to look at him.

"That wasn't a true mating," he replied. "Next time, my body will gain the enjoyment. This time, my heart knew the pleasure."

She studied his handsome face, and was very content with what she saw. It was not so much the sheer beauty of his male face that attracted her, but the honesty and integrity in his eyes. She sensed the honor in this man and knew he had spoken the truth to his friend at the inn, "*I would like this woman as my life-mate.*"

Not, she thought, as she lost herself in his golden gaze, as a broodmare or a harlot to ride when the itch struck, but as one to spend the rest of his years beside.

"Would we be equal partners?" she asked softly.

"Equal partners in what, wench?" he asked, stifling a yawn.

"Should we to become life-mates."

Leksi's eyebrows shot up. "You would consider it?"

"Are you proposing?"

"Would you accept if I did?"

"Best to ask then find out, don't you think, warrior?" she countered.

"I thought you hated all men and had no use for us."

Kynthia shrugged, and turned over to lie on her back. She placed her arms beneath her head and looked up at the night sky. "Are you going to ask me or not?"

He was staring at her lush breasts, bare to the moonlight and glistening with a sheen of perspiration. He reached out and laid his palm on one firm globe, and kneaded gently.

"What will your aunt and sisters think?"

"They will be glad they will no longer have to waylay strangers in an attempt to find me a man," she said with a sigh.

"They will accept me?"

Kynthia was becoming aroused again as his hand worked its magic on her breast.

"They brought you to me in the first place, didn't they?"

"Aye, but I wasn't the nicest of visitors," he muttered.

"As a man being pillaged, you acquitted yourself well enough. I think they found you cute."

Leksi snorted. "I should have had each of them thrown into a dungeon with other rapists," he groused.

"You would not have and you know it," she said with a grin. "What man would admit being taken by force by a woman or two?"

"One intent on bragging, I suppose," he said, and leaned over to press his lips around her nipple.

Kynthia sighed with pleasure, and removed one arm from under her head so she could run her fingers through the silk of his thick hair.

"You know," she said, as the heat began building in her cunt once more, "they had never allowed a male to escape before you."

"Um," he said, laving her nipple. He flicked it with his tongue then lightly grazed it with his teeth.

"It was either sell them to the Amazeens or the Hell Hags, but you were different."

"How come?" he asked, as he moved his attention to the other nipple.

"Aunt Galatea most likely decided you were the one, else she would never have suckled you."

He stopped and looked up at her. "Is that going to be a problem should we become life-mates?"

"Aunt Galatea?"

"Aye."

"I think not. She approves of you," Kynthia replied. "I think she gave you her seal of endorsement, don't you?"

"I suppose you could say that," he said, withdrawing from her luscious breasts. He was about to push his breeches down over his hips when a discreet clearing of the throat snapped his head sideways.

Kratos was standing where the wolf had been lying. Arms akimbo, he was looking up at the night sky, studiously avoiding looking at the naked woman lying beside Leksi.

"What the hell are you doing out here?" Leksi demanded. He got to his feet and began buttoning up his breeches despite the stiff erection that threatened to poke through the fabric.

"Lord Krull has called in all the men. We have a situation in Pleiades," Kratos answered, finding something even more interesting than the night sky as he studied a date palm close beside him.

"Now?" Leksi moaned. "Why the hell now?"

Kratos risked looking at his young friend. "I suppose I could go back and ask him to delay whatever it is he thinks is important until you dip your wick, Helios. Think you he will be understanding?"

Leksi cursed beneath his breath. He looked about him for his shirt and picked what he thought was his clothing, and thrust his arms through the sleeves, frowning as he tried to button it.

"I think that belongs to the lady," Kratos said with a chuckle that pretended to be a cough.

Kynthia sat up—unconcerned by her nudity and unsure why—and snagged her own breeches. "Is there a border war brewing, Lord Kratos?" she asked, remembering the name the warrior had termed this very striking man.

Kratos smiled, greatly entertained at the sight of her nudity. "Aye, Lady Kynthia, I believe 'tis."

As she stepped into her breeches, Kynthia glanced at Leksi. "Was that why you were in Qabala? Were you trying to arrange a truce between Ventura and the Pleiadesians?"

"For what good it did me," Leksi said. He stuffed his shirt into his breeches. "The Qabalans are afraid of their own shadow. They refused to get involved."

"Well, they have always been neutral during any of the wars," Kynthia defended.

"They are noncommittal, evasive, irritatingly vague shitheads," Leksi snapped.

"But they make an excellent cheese," Kratos observed.

Kynthia hid a smile behind her hand. "Perhaps my sisters and I could be of some assistance to you. We have reason to hate the Pleiadesians."

Leksi looked around. "Are you offering the help of the Amazeen?"

"The Daughters of the Night, as well," Kynthia said. "Queen Mona of the Bandarese has ample reason to hate King Abalam of Pleiades. Her daughter Lilit, even more so."

"I've heard strange tales of Princess Lilit," Kratos commented.

"Aye," Kynthia agreed. "She is power-hungry and when her mother dies, I think the Daughters will be led in a new direction if Lilit has her way."

"I will need to run this by Lord Krull, but I imagine he would welcome all the help he can get against King Abalam. The Akkadians are keeping out of it along with the Qabalans so we're up against a force greater than our own as it is."

"The Akkadians are in the midst of their own civil war," Kynthia pointed out. "Now is not the time to ask for their help."

Leksi shrugged. "There has never been any love lost between Akkadia and Ventura."

"I will ride back to my aunt's villa and have her call an assembly. She sits on the Council of the Elders and her word is held in high esteem," Kynthia said, making for her mount.

"Aren't you forgetting something, wench?" Leksi called out.

Kynthia looked around. "What?"

"Did you not ask me if I intended to do something?"

Kynthia glanced at Kratos then back to her lover. "Aye," she said.

"Then consider the question asked," Leksi said.

Narrowing her eyes, Kynthia put her hands on her hips. "No," she said, shaking her head. "That is not the way it will play out, warrior."

Leksi frowned. "You want me on my knees?"

Kratos puckered his lips in a silent whistle, and looked from the warrior to the lady then back again.

"I will have it done properly," Kynthia agreed.

Rolling his eyes and throwing his hands to the heavens, Leksi strode to her, stopped, and then went gracefully to one knee. Reaching out, he took her left hand in his and put his right hand over his heart.

"Lady Kynthia, will you Join with me and become my life-mate?" he asked.

Kynthia grinned. "Aye, Lord Leksi Helios, I pledge myself to you as your life-mate."

"So be it," Leksi said, and released her hand. "When this present situation has been remedied, we will plight our troth."

"We will," she agreed and put her shirt back on. She nodded and without another word, un-hobbled her steed and swung atop the restless beast. With a curt bob of her head to Kratos, she kicked Aeolus into motion and was soon lost in the dark shadows of the desert.

"By the gods, boy," Kratos said, his voice rife with admiration. "I believe you have plucked the cream of the crop there. She is as lovely as you claimed her to be."

"Let's get this war over with so I can claim her in reality, old friend," Leksi said then realized he had forgotten to bring a mount of his own when he had returned Kynthia's.

"Up for a run, are you?" Kratos remarked as he headed for his horse.

Chapter Six

"It requires a meeting of the combined assemblies," Galatea explained, "but I doubt any of the Sisters will gainsay a temporary alliance with Ventura if it means ridding the land of Abalam."

"The Daughters might balk at helping," Celadina said. "The Hell Hags are a breed unto their own."

"Aye, but Queen Mona has been known to spend time incognito in Ventura during the Festival of Spring," Ophelia commented. "Some say that is how Lilit came to be."

"Lilit," Haidee said with a frown. "I've heard it was a demon that sired her. She is a bloodthirsty child."

"A child not more than a year or so younger than you," Erinyes remarked.

"Four years younger," Haidee said. "And has yet to have her first monthly."

"How would you know?" Erinyes questioned.

"Must you question everything I say, Erinyes?" Haidee threw at her sister. "I spent two months in Bandar, remember? I was forced to sleep beside that miserable little bitch. She told me she would be glad when she had her first flow for then all her power would come to her."

"What power?" Celadina asked.

"How would I know?" Haidee snapped. "I tried not to talk to that witch any more than I had to." She shot her aunt a disgusted look. "I wasn't there of my own accord."

"No, but you were there to represent the Ancaeus family," Galatea reminded her niece. "Well, at least the female side of it even though my sister—the gods rest her burdened soul—was never allowed to make the trek to the Gatherings once she married that illiterate ass."

"Speaking of the illiterate ass, have you visited our father and brother of late, Kynthia?" Erinyes asked.

Kynthia shot her sister a nasty look. "No, why should I? Have you?"

"No reason to," Erinyes replied. "Like you, I am well rid of those barbarians."

"You had best be thankful our laws do not require you to be re-dowered as do the Venturian and Akkadian laws," Galatea said. "Else you would be back on the marriage auction block and not free to come and go as you do here."

"Father and his simpleton son can go to hell for all I care," Erinyes said. "They have made their last copper piece off me!" She turned to Ophelia. "But you? You are different. They might remember you never wed that handsome boy, Phaon, and strike for another betrothal."

"They won't," Kynthia stated. When the others looked at her, she shrugged. "They know I'd never allow it. If Ophelia wants a man, it's up to her to find him."

Galatea tilted her head to one side. "As you found Lord Leksi?"

"All right!" Kynthia grated. "I admit you had a hand in putting the two of us together, but it was not your doing that sealed the deal!"

With that said, Kynthia stalked off to her room.

"The Venturian is going to have his hands full with Kynthia," Celadina said.

"I still can't believe she gave in on this one," Haidee said. "What makes this man different than all the others we brought to her?"

"Did you get a good look at his cock?" Erinyes asked. "That alone should have been enough."

"It wasn't the strength and length of his cock that won our Kynthia's heart," Galatea said, surprising the others who looked at her with wide eyes. "Aye, you heard me right—he won her heart."

"By going up through her cunt apparently," Erinyes scoffed.

"Perhaps," Galatea agreed, "but since that was the crux of her problem with men to begin with, I believe he handled her just as the gods meant for him to."

* * * * *

Leksi was miserable as he pretended to listen to the Lord High Commander of the Venturian Forces detail the plan to subdue King Abalam. The warrior's mind was on the lovely woman he had yet to make his own though he knew he had pleasured her quite well and—in the doing—won her affection. His hands itched to hold her again and his tool throbbed with the desire to plunge—

"Helios, are you listening to me?" Lord Konan Krull bellowed.

Leksi jumped, his face hot with embarrassment. "Aye, Your Grace. I have heard every word!"

Lord Krull's midnight black eyes narrowed. "Then you will agree to the assignment for which I just asked for a volunteer?"

Swallowing, for in truth he had not heard his commander's request, the warrior dared not look at those around him—and especially not Kratos—so stared straight ahead as he replied, "Aye, Your Grace. I will accept the assignment."

"Fool," Leksi heard Kratos say under his breath.

Wondering what it was he'd gotten himself into, the warrior forced his attention back to Lord Krull.

"As soon as Helios has completed his part of the plan, we will ride into Nebul, take Abalam hostage and place our stalwart warrior upon the throne as Princess Clea's consort."

83

Leksi frowned. What stalwart warrior, he wondered? When the implication hit him, his eyes flared wide and his mouth dropped open.

"You've stepped in it this time," Kratos mumbled out of the side of his mouth. "You can kiss the lovely Kynthia goodbye."

Slowly Leksi turned his horrified gaze to Kratos. "To what did I agree?" he whispered, terrified of the answer.

"If you will remember," Lord Krull said, strolling down the ranks to where Leksi stood at the head of his regiment of troops, "I asked for a volunteer to take the Princess Clea to wife." He stared at Leksi. "You did agree to the assignment, didn't you? That *was* what you agreed, wasn't it?"

"Aye, Your Grace, but—" Leksi began.

"And you also will remember me saying that only with the production of a suitable heir of joint Pleiadesian and Venturian offspring would the troubles between our two countries ever cease and that whoever took the assignment must agree to get Clea with child as quickly as possible."

Risking a look at Kratos, who stood beside him, Leksi could see pity etched on the older man's craggy face. The warrior's shoulders slumped for he had gotten himself into unbelievable trouble.

"You weren't listening, were you?" Lord Krull asked.

Leksi shook his head. "No, Your Grace. I was not."

"So, now you must pay the price for your woolgathering, eh?"

Nodding miserably, Leksi dug his fingernails into the palms of his hands. "Aye, Your Grace. My humblest apologies."

Krull stood in front of his second in command and glared at him. The legendary warrior towered over Leksi's six-foot-two-inch height and his muscular body made Leksi look almost effeminate. With strong hands—the knuckles of which bore scars from many a fistfight—planted on his lean hips, the Lord High Commander of the Venturian Forces had the undivided of attention of every soldier in the room.

"What thoughts had claimed your mind and caused you to ignore my words, Helios?" Lord Krull demanded.

Leksi knew better than to compound his sin with another lie. "A woman, Your Grace."

There was a smattering of snickering among the troops but Lord Krull's piercing black gaze swept over the assemblage and the snickers ceased. When he was satisfied no obvious humor remained, he turned his hawk-like glare back to Leksi. "What woman?" he asked.

"Lady Kynthia Ancaeus," Leksi replied.

"I do not know this woman," Lord Krull stated. "From where does she come?"

"Near the Qabala border, Your Grace."

Another rumble of sound shifted over the troops and once more Lord Krull surveyed the room. His eyes were fierce and not one man there could meet that steady gaze.

"Near the Qabala border," Lord Krull said. "On Amazeen lands?"

"Nay, Your Grace, but near there."

"On Hell Hag lands?"

Leksi sighed. "Nay, Your Grace, but close to there, as well."

"I see. Am I to understand you met this woman when you took it upon yourself to try to gain the help of those sissified Qabalans?"

"Aye, Your Grace."

Lord Krull was silent for a long time. He clasped his hands behind his back and walked the length of the formation then turned and walked back to where Leksi stood at attention. He was in front of the third man down from the warrior, his back to Leksi, when Krull asked if it was at the villa of Galatea Atredides that he met the lady.

Leksi flinched, but was unable to answer for his mouth had gone suddenly dry.

"Captain Helios?" Lord Krull asked. "Did you hear my question or were you woolgathering again?" The Lord High Commander turned and locked his stare on Leksi.

"Aye," Leksi managed to croak. "Aye, Your Grace. I believe that is the lady's name."

"And did you meet her nieces by any chance?"

Kratos flicked his gaze to Leksi. "Answer him, boy!" he hissed.

Knowing Lord Konan Krull somehow knew about Galatea Atredides and her band of Mad Rapists, Leksi hung his head. "Aye, Your Grace. I met them."

Krull turned and walked back to his second in command. He came toe-to-toe with the warrior. "What I said while you were daydreaming of Galatea's niece was that it was too bad we couldn't get someone to marry that cow of a bitch Clea, Abalam's daughter. I said that were such a stupid man be found to take on that assignment, I would guarantee him a seat on the throne beside Clea if he would but get her with child. Under such circumstances, she would be forced into Joining with that warrior, making him her consort, and thus assuring peace between Pleiades and Ventura."

Leksi stumbled back as his commander crowded into him even more.

"It was said in jest, Helios," Lord Krull snarled. "It was never meant to be a true mission but since you volunteered for it, I suppose we will go ahead and send you."

Leksi groaned. He had, indeed, stepped in it this time.

"Or would you rather return to Galatea's villa and visit a while with her nieces?"

Leksi stared at his commander. "You know?" he whispered.

"What goes on there?" Krull asked. "Aye, I've known for years, but this is the first time I've learned a Venturian has spent time at Atredides' villa." He waved a dismissive hand. "What happens to Akkadians and Qabalans are of no concern to me, and if a Pleiadesian winds up in Galatea's hands, all the better!" He leaned forward and put his mouth to Leksi's ear. "Did you enjoy your sojourn with them?"

"Nay, Your Grace," Leksi said truthfully.

Lord Krull cocked an eyebrow. "Not even with the lovely Kynthia for whom I am told those bitches are seeking a mate?"

"Well," Leksi said. "That is another matter, Your Grace."

Krull straightened. There was a gleam in his eye and he half-smiled at Leksi. "Well, now, it's like that, is it?"

"I have asked her to be my life-mate, Your Grace, and she has pledged herself to me."

"I see. Well, congratulations, Captain. Too bad you won't be able to keep your part of the bargain, eh?"

Leksi was stunned as his commander pivoted and walked off. "But, Your Grace!" he called out.

Krull spun around. "You agreed to my hypothetical assignment, did you not?"

All eyes were on Leksi, and the warrior was sweating profusely. He could see his future with Kynthia rapidly vanishing and he felt the grief of it to the marrow of his soul.

"You don't want to marry Princess Clea?" Krull challenged.

"Nay, Your Grace," Leksi replied.

"Nor sit the throne of Pleiades beside her?"

"Nay, Your Grace."

"Or produce half-Pleiadesian, half-Venturian brats to seal a lasting peace between the two countries?"

"The thought of mating with Princess Clea..." Leksi began, shuddering, "...is a horror to me, Your Grace."

"Nor carry out an assignment I gave you and for which you volunteered of your own accord?" Krull asked with his eyes narrowed dangerously.

Trapped, Leksi hung his head. "I have no choice but to do as you bid for I was foolish and was not paying attention. It is your right to punish me, Your Grace, and if that is your decision, so be it. I will make good on my vow and see the assignment through to completion."

"Even though you will lose your lady and your freedom?"

"Aye, Your Grace," Leksi said in a defeated voice.

"Too bad I don't intend to hold you to it, eh, Captain?" Krull inquired, and when Leksi looked up, the Lord High Commander grinned. "Unless, of course, you would prefer Clea's distinctive looks to those of Kynthia Ancaeus."

Laughter rang out over the assemblage and Kratos broke ranks to slap Leksi on the back. Such was the ease with which Krull's men held him, other soldiers came to mill around Leksi and shove him good-naturedly for his folly.

"So, Clea won't gain the handsome Captain Helios to husband, but we still need a plan to get into the keep and take Abalam," Lord Krull said. "Let's meet back here at nine of the clock tomorrow morn. I will expect a plan by then, gentlemen."

Kratos slipped an arm around Leksi's shoulders. "You do realize he could well have held you to your vow, don't you, brat?"

"Aye," Leksi answered, looking across the room to where Lord Krull was deep in conversation with a Tribunal member.

"What was that all about concerning the villa where you met your lady? Is there something I should know about there?" Kratos inquired.

"I'll tell you someday, old friend," Leksi replied.

Kratos lowered his voice. "Has it to do with your lady being a shape shifter?"

Leksi glanced around but no one was close enough to hear. "That is a secret it would be dangerous to her for others to know, Kratos."

Pressing his index finger and thumb together, Kratos imitated sealing his lips. "Not from this mouth will anyone hear of it, Leksi."

"Good man," Leksi said. "Now let's go speak with Lord Krull, and extend my lady's offer to him. Perhaps I know of a way we can gain Abalam's keep and take that troublemaker into custody."

Chapter Seven

King Abalam Robeus was an evil man. No one disputed that fact and those who had reason to observe his evil up close swore he was not only evil but wickedness personified.

As ugly as he was evil, his malevolence stabbed from beady little eyes that resembled those of a pig. Grossly fat, he had stubby little fingers—each adorned with a large, expensive ring—and feet so small it was hard for him to stand. With flabby jowls that wobbled as he talked, flesh the color of mottled clay and legs so bowed a good-sized boulder could pass between them and not touch either knee. There was nothing in the least appealing about the king.

His daughter was just as unattractive as he but in a different way.

Reed-thin and overly tall, with a face as sharp as a razor, huge eyes that watered constantly beneath sparse eyebrows that formed one long line across the top of her beak-like nose, bony hips that protruded against even the most expensive gowns, huge, flat feet that slapped the floor as she walked and a peculiarly bad odor that clung to her even fresh from a long soak, Clea Robeus was a very unenviable person.

But her pitiful ugliness did not mirror her soul for she was of a sweet, charitable disposition and bore a wicked sense of humor—telling jokes even at her own expense—that often set the somber, terrified court to laughing.

"Never will I find a man to Join with me unless his life depends upon it," she said often, followed by, "Even then I imagine he would prefer death to my bony embrace."

Since his daughter did not share his penchant for evil, the king ignored Clea as faithfully as he had fucked her hapless mother thirty-nine years earlier. He could not have cared less if she ever snared a mate and certainly would never put himself — or his court — to the trouble to find her one.

"Let the gods-awful hag wither and die for all I care," King Abalam had been heard to say. "Had she been a male child, I might have given a shit, but what good is a female but to hump, and not even I would lay hands to that bitch!"

Sitting with her ladies-in-waiting, Clea was hard at work on a tapestry that depicted the Great War between Pleiades and Ventura. Though neither country had won the war, both sides had lost thousands upon thousands of its inhabitants and many heroes had been born upon the battlefields.

"Ah, Your Grace, that is a very elegant rendering of Lord Konan Krull," Marbas, one of Clea's ladies-in-waiting proclaimed as she came to view the progress her princess had made on the tapestry.

"Aye, but he is a handsome man, is he not?" Clea asked with a heartfelt sigh. "So tall and brave and does he not sit his destrier well?"

"Who is that warrior?" Marbas asked. She pointed to a young man holding two soldiers at bay with his mighty sword.

"Lord Leksi Helios, son of Sirius. He, too, is quite the chevalier, eh?"

"Very handsome, Your Grace, but not as wickedly beautiful as the Lord High Commander."

"Nor as brutal as Krull," Clea commented as she adjusted the tapestry stand to alleviate the ache in her shoulders. "Though I am told he is the very gentlest of lovers with his wife, the Lady Isabell."

"Oh, to be the mate of such gallant men," Marbas said with a heavy sigh.

"You will find a husband one day, Mari. Have no fear of it."

Clea had run out of yarn for her needle so she sat back in her chair and picked up a skein. Her eyesight was fading as she grew older and the condition that caused her eyes to water constantly made her squint, thus deepening the creases in her face.

"When you are queen, do you think you could find me a mate who is as handsome as Lord Krull?" Marbas asked.

Her mistress laughed. "I doubt me there are any men quite as handsome as that one, but I will do my best to find you one who will be a good husband to you and…" She lowered her voice. "A very skilled lover!"

Marbas blushed and ducked her head.

"Milady, might Lord Nergal have a moment of your time?" Sariel, another of the ladies-in-waiting asked.

Clea looked up to find one of her father's toadies standing poised in the doorway. She frowned deeply for the man was one she loathed. "Aye, Lord Nergal?" she ground out.

"His Majesty has issued an order that you are to remain in your quarters for the coming week," Lord Nergal stated.

Laying her hands in her lap, Clea stared at her father's Chief of the Secret Police and consigned him to the very depths of the Abyss. Each time she was forced to look upon Nergal, she felt queasiness in the pit of her stomach.

"May I ask why I am being relegated once more to my quarters and not allowed the freedom of the keep, Lord Nergal?"

Though his extraordinarily striking features turned the heads of beautiful women who were not aware of his despicable proclivities, Nergal preferred the company of less comely females with whom he felt he did not have to compete. With the Princess, he felt superior, and his manner and tone suggested as much. Despite the fact she was of royal heritage and in direct line to the throne of Pleiades, he did not feel she was due even a modicum of respect since her father showed her none, himself.

"If he had wanted you to know, he would have given me permission to tell you," Nergal snapped.

"And, naturally, you would have been overjoyed to give me his reason, wouldn't you, Lord Nergal?" Clea returned.

"Keep yourself to your quarters, woman, and do not question the motives of your king. Best you keep to female things like that hideous tapestry you seem too unskilled to complete," Lord Nergal said.

The women around Clea gasped at the man's audacity and looked to their lady, expecting her to chastise the offender. But Clea picked up her tapestry needle and thread, and kept silent.

"You," Nergal said with a grunt, pointing at Marbas. "Come to my quarters at half-past the hour." He turned and started to walk away but Clea's voice stopped him.

"She is suffering from the pox, Lord Nergal. Do you still wish her to come to your bed?"

Lord Nergal turned around and glared at the king's daughter. His handsome features were tight with disgust. Without another word, he spun around and marched off.

"Milady, he will go to the Healer and—"

"And the Healer will tell him that each of Princess Clea's ladies-in-waiting are pox-riddled," Clea assured her. "I have greased his filthy palm many times over to save you women the curse of being mauled by a piece of offal like Sorath Nergal!"

Marbas rushed to her mistress and knelt down beside her, wrapping her hands around Clea's scrawny legs. "Thank you, Your Grace. Oh, thank you!"

Clea put a hand to the girl's dark hair. "We will save your virginal offering to a man worthy to claim it, Mari. I swear that to you on my beloved mother's grave."

"I wish the Venturians had won the war," Sariel stated. "With a man like Lord Krull at the head of our Tribunal, the women of Pleiades would not have to suffer at the hands of men like Lord Nergal."

"I, too, wish they had won the war, Sariel," Clea told her. "Perhaps one day those powerful warriors will march on Nebul and free us all."

"But would you be allowed to keep the throne, Your Grace?" Marbas questioned.

Clea continued to stroke Marbas' hair. Her rheumy eyes gazed into the distance. "I don't see why not. I am no threat to them, and I believe I would make a good monarch."

"The best," Marbas swore. "The very best, milady!"

"Then let's say our prayers that one day the gods will take pity on us and rid us of the wickedness that prevails in our land," Clea advised her women.

"Come to us, Lord Krull," Sariel pleaded, her hands clasped to her chin. "Come and deliver us from the evil in which we are forced to live."

"Come, Leksi," Clea whispered, her gaze shifting to the man who visited her often in her secret dreams. "Come and rescue me."

Chapter Eight

Kynthia tossed upon her bed and flung the covers this way and that. She was restless in her sleep for an age-old nightmare had come to gallop across her memory, its pounding hooves striking to the rhythm of her terrified heart.

In her dreams, she was running upon the Isle of Uaigneas, trying to outdistance the gruesome thing racing toward her. She ran through the forest with tree limbs slapping at her face, she stumbled over logs and fell face down in the blistering sand. Looking behind her, she could see the loathsome entity slithering after her and she got up and ran again, the stitch in her side so painful she moaned in her sleep. For what felt like hours, she raced through the forest until she came to the high cliff overlooking the island where the Reaper's airship, *The Levant*, sat perched like a mighty black raptor.

There was nowhere else to run. All avenues of escape were closed off to her and when she dared to look around one last time, she was horrified to find the thing from which she had been striving to escape loaming over her, wicked talons curled, and flashing incisors dripping with saliva, glowing red eyes piercing her to the marrow of her bones. She could either accept the evil coming at her or turn and jump from the cliff to the jagged rocks far below. The decision was hers.

"It is your choice, wench," Cainer Cree's voice came at her from the sky.

And she had made her decision by holding her arms out to the creature and offering her neck to its wicked fangs. As the sharpness hooked into her flesh, Kynthia Ancaeus sank to the ground in unconscious worship of the Transition she knew would soon come.

With a gasp, Kynthia sat up in the bed. Her legs were tangled in the rumpled sheets and she viciously kicked them away, unnerved by the restriction that had wound its way around her ankles. Shivering, her teeth chattering, she plastered herself to the headboard and drew her knees up, wrapped her arms around them, and sat there rocking back and forth, a soft keening sound issuing from her constricted throat as her backbone thumped against the wooden slats of the headboard.

"It was your choice, wench," she thought she heard the Reaper say.

"I know," Kynthia muttered. "I know it was."

Yet there were times she bitterly regretted accepting the parasite from Cainer Cree.

"You will need to harvest it from my back," the Reaper explained. "There is a small jug into which you will drop the fledgling. Be quick and cover the jug for it will strive to escape."

"How big is the thing inside you?" she asked.

"The Queen is about a foot long. She is coiled around her hive of about four-dozen nestlings. All you need to gather is one of them."

"But how will I—"

"You won't be able to miss it once you cut me open," he interrupted. "The Queen looks like an organ and you won't see either her head or her tail. The nestlings are eel-like, squirming things which are in a honeycombed sac attached to my kidney."

Kynthia felt nauseous. "Will the parasite I harvest from you grow to be as big as the Queen inside you?"

"Aye."

"Inside me," Kynthia whispered. "Such things will grow inside me."

"Aye, wench. Inside you."

That evening, she had dreamed of the horror coming at her for the first time and when she had awoke screaming, she had found herself wrapped tightly in the Reaper's arms, his soothing voice calming her as she clung to him.

"It is your choice, Kynthia. Do not make it unless you are totally committed to this. You have the freedom to walk away from what I am offering," he told her.

"No," she said, shaking her head. "I want this."

She had fallen asleep in his arms and her dreams had changed drastically. Instead of fleeing to the brink of death upon the cliff, she was running happily toward Cainer Cree, his beckoning arms wide. Gladly she had gone into those arms and felt them close around her.

He swung her up in his brawny arms and carried her to his hut. There, he laid her upon his solitary bunk and with the wave of his hands, freed her of her clothing. In the beat of a heart, his vanished from his heavily muscled frame as his knee pressed into the mattress and he straddled her.

She could feel the heat and weight of his staff as it lay against her thigh. Closing her eyes to his knowing hands as they kneaded her breasts and his strong fingers plucked at her nipples, she reached down to grasp that steely tool.

He was warm in her hands and throbbing, as hard as stone in her hand. Looking past his muscular forearms, she stared at the thick veins than ran the length of his cock. There was power in those veins and she ran the tip of her finger down one crooked length.

"It is your choice, Kynthia," he whispered to her, and that mighty weapon leapt in her hand.

She held her arms out to him and he lowered his body to hers. The weight of him was delicious, his scent one of heady potency. As he settled atop her, he claimed her mouth with his and did wickedly delectable things with his quick tongue. His hands were on her hips then sliding beneath her to cup her ass. She could feel his fingers digging lightly into her flesh and reveled in the sensation.

His cock was throbbing against her clit and she opened her legs as he moved to position his legs between hers.

"It is your choice," he repeated, and his staff stirred against her, straining to thrust inside her welcoming slit.

She arched her back and threw her legs around his hips, anchoring him to her. Once more, she felt his cock pressing against her vaginal lips. She strained toward him, granting him permission to take her.

But it was not his cock that thrust inside her.

It was the triangular green head of the Queen that snaked her way inside Kynthia's cunt. The thick, horny scales ripped at the tender flesh and tore open the walls of her vagina as the beastess drove deeper inside Kynthia's shuddering body.

Screams of agony ripped from a throat half-paralyzed with fear and disgust. Writhing upon the bed, she tried to buck off the creature impaling her for the Reaper's handsome face had melted into the leering, deadly stare of something not of this world.

"It was your choice," the creature taunted, and with one brutal, savage thrust drove its body deep into Kynthia. As it did, it became one long, snakelike thing that vanished into her depths, its forked tail the last thing she saw disappearing inside her before spiraling into unconsciousness.

"Kynthia, wake!"

The Reaper's voice seem to be coming from the heavens when in truth he was right beside her, his arms wrapped tightly around her. When she opened her eyes and looked up into his stern face, she started thrashing, pushing against him in an effort to escape. When he would not let go of her, she began to scream mindlessly and lash out at him with her fists. She heard one annoyed sigh then saw the stars come down from the heavens as he gave her a light tap that immediately brought her out of her frenzy.

"Behave," he warned, and tightened his arms around her.

Shaking her head to send the stars back to the cosmos, she began to cry. "I'm sorry!" she burst out.

He crooned to her in a language she did not know and suspected was his native tongue from that world far beyond her own. It was lyrical and bore a decided similarity to Chalean High Speech. As he spoke, he calmly smoothed her hair and rocked her gently against him.

"I am so ashamed," she blubbered.

"For what?" he inquired. "Having wicked dreams of me?"

She looked up at him. "You read my thoughts?" she accused.

"How could I not when they were so strong, Sweeting?"

Pushing away from him, she ran the sleeve of her blouse under her nose. "I didn't mean to have such evil dreams of you."

"Of course, you didn't, and the dream really wasn't about me."

"It wasn't?"

"No. It was partially the need you have for a man's body to satisfy you and—"

"I want no such thing!"

He held up a hand, forestalling any further denials. "And partially the fear of taking on the parasite."

"Had you but known what would happen to you, would you not have feared it, Reaper?" she challenged.

"I had no choice. You do."

"So you keep telling me," she snapped.

"Are you still sure that is what you wish to do?"

"Aye, I am very sure. But that part about me wanting a man—"

"One day, you will meet a man whose hand will start a fire in your loins, milady. His gentlest touch will stoke that fire until it is a blazing inferno only his male potency can extinguish.

When you find such a man, hold fast to him for you will know you have found your life-mate."

"Aye, well, how will I know such a man when I happen upon him?" she sneered.

"You will know him by his honesty and his honor. He will vow never to hurt you," he replied. "Nor will he ever allow anyone or anything to hurt you. He will swear to cherish you, as you deserve to be cherished. That is how you will know."

"Humph," Kynthia snorted. "I'll believe that when I find such a mythical creature."

"Like dragons, they do exist, wench," the Reaper said with a glint in his golden eyes.

* * * * *

Sitting pressed to the headboard of her bed in Aunt Galatea's villa, Kynthia closed her eyes. "Reaper?" she asked. "Are you there?"

Where else would I be? came an amused whisper.

Kynthia smiled. "I found him, just as you said I would."

Aye, and he seems a good man.

"I think he wants to become One with the Blood."

I gleaned as much, but he might be more concerned with being than with being.

Kynthia frowned. "I don't understand."

He knows there is strength in a Reaper, and the warrior in him sees that as a powerful benefit. The politician in him sees the ability to read minds as an advantage. With the capability of nearly instantaneous healing, the inability to catch illnesses and a Reaper's natural longevity, the pragmatic in him sees more positive than negative things in the changing.

"Rather than simply wanting to be my mate and spend his lifetime with me?" she offered.

He wants those things, too, wench, but he is a practical man, and practicality will always come first with him even though his heart is firmly in your keeping.

"You think so?"

I know so.

"So should I have him harvest one of my nestlings?"

It is your decision to make, Kynthia. Only you can decide.

Kynthia sighed. She knew he would say no more about Leksi Helios' desire to be One with the Blood. "Have you made any more like us?"

There was a long moment of silence then the Reaper's tone was harsh when he replied.

Only a few and only one to whom I am exceedingly sorry I gave it. He has made many more like us and not a one of them is worthy of the positive things the changeling can accomplish.

"Who is he? Should I be concerned about him?"

No. His days are numbered. Leave his punishment to the gods for it will surely come with a vengeance. Those he made will vanish from the face of the earth.

She sensed him pulling away and let him go. She pictured him sitting on the cliff, staring out at his beloved airship and dreaming dreams of yesteryears when he was not the strange recluse on the Isle of Uaignes.

* * * * *

Lord Krull swirled his goblet of Chalean brandy and stared down into the potent amber liquid. He had been silent for half an hour and both Leksi and Kratos knew better than to interrupt whatever thoughts the Lord High Commander was reading in the fiery liquor.

"I met Queen Mona a few years ago," Krull finally said. "She seems a very competent woman though that daughter of hers makes my balls tighten."

"I've heard rumors that the daughter was sired by a demon," Kratos commented.

"That doesn't surprise me in the least," the Lord High Commander said, taking a sip of his brandy. "She had a fierce, nasty look about her and kept staring at me as though I was a confection on a dessert trencher, and there I was near to four times her age."

Leksi wiggled in his chair. "There are some females who mature early, Your Grace. Perhaps she is one of them."

"Well, such lascivious thoughts I sensed from that child would unsettle any grown man lest he be one who likes to diddle children," Krull said.

"Have you met the Amazeen queens?" Kratos inquired.

"No, and I don't care to," Krull said, draining his goblet.

"For the life of me," Leksi said, "I do not understand why they need two queens."

"One is for defense and the other for domestic issues," Krull commented. "It seems strange to us but seems to work for them. Queen Deianeira is the defense queen. Her twin sister, Antianeira, is the domestic queen. I have heard they are beauties with hair of flame but with only one breast."

"Legend has it that at puberty the Amazeens have their right breasts removed," Kratos explained. "Unless she is left-handed and then it's her left breast."

"Why?" Leksi asked, his forehead crinkled.

"The better to pull a bowstring," Krull answered for Kratos.

"Oh," Leksi said.

"So your lady thinks she can bring both the Daughters of the Night and the Amazeen to be our allies," Krull stated. "Do you think she can pull it off, Helios?"

"She told me both the Daughters and the Amazeen have reason to hate the Pleiadesians."

"You know why, don't you?" Krull queried.

Both Leksi and Kratos shook their heads.

Krull leaned back in his chair and put his booted feet on the top of his desk then crossed his ankles. Lacing his fingers together, he put them behind his head. "I found out about it from Queen Mona, herself," he said. "She was in Akkadia asking for help from those sons-of-bitches but King Asshole refused."

Leksi and Kratos exchanged an amused glance. They knew with what contempt their commander held King Ashbrolen of Akkadia.

"Back around the time King Jordyle took the throne of Ventura there was a squadron of Hell Hags escorting a group of novitiates to the Abbey of Marpesia in Bandar. In route, they were attacked by a party of Nebullian storm troopers."

"They were a long way from the border," Leksi said.

"Obviously they were looking for trouble and found it with the Witches of Bandar. The Hell Hags acquitted themselves well enough—slaying all but three of the fifteen storm troopers—but all save one of the novitiates was killed during the melee. The one who remained was Queen Mona's niece and the surviving storm troopers made off with her."

"That had to have infuriated the Witches," Leksi said.

"For the most part, the Daughters of the Night were not warrior women back then. They were mystics, healers, the teachers of children. So, Queen Mona asked the Amazeens for help. Their defense queen sent a force of women to try to catch the storm troopers before they crossed back into Pleiades, but there was an ambush and not one of the Amazeen survived the attack. The bastards raped the women as they lay dying then took their remaining breasts as trophies.

"Left with having to bed King Abalam for her niece's return, Queen Mona sent word to him. As you can imagine, he laughed at the note and sent word back that he had every intention of keeping the girl there for his own amusement. She was but twelve at the time."

"Bastard," Kratos snarled.

"So Queen Mona went to the Akkadians. I was there as a representative of our new King and listened to her petition before the Akkadian High Council. When they turned her down, I followed her outside and offered my assistance."

Leksi and Kratos sat straighter in their chairs. "Did King Jordyle know you had done this?" Leksi asked.

Krull shook his head, a half-smile on his darkly tanned face. "Nay, and if he had it wouldn't have stayed my offer. At the time, my youngest daughter had just turned twelve."

"Did you go to Nebul?"

"I was almost to the border when a lone rider came galloping toward me. She was an emissary from Queen Mona. She gave me a handwritten note from the Queen. In the note, she bid me return to Tasjorn for her niece had been returned to Bandar."

"Dead?" Leksi asked quietly.

"Aye and mutilated beyond belief except for her face. Abalam had left that intact so the child could be recognized."

Kratos narrowed his eyes. "You went on to Nebul anyway, didn't you?"

"I knew I'd never get near enough to Abalam to take him, but our spies in Nebul found out who the men were who had taken the child," Krull replied. His smile widened. "I sent their heads—intact, so they would be recognized—to Queen Mona."

Leksi whistled. "So she owes you now."

Krull shook his head. "She doesn't owe me anything, Helios. What I did, I did for the child. She needed to be avenged."

"Nevertheless, she should help us get that psychotic demon. If ever a man deserves to die an agonizing death, it is Abalam Robeus!" Leksi growled.

"Bring him to the dungeons here at the keep and I'll make that death last a long, long time," Kratos stated.

The Lord High Commander looked at his lieutenant. "I'll hold you to that, Kratos Hesar."

"Consider it done, Your Grace!"

* * * * *

Queen Mona of Bandar listened quietly as the Council of Elders heard the petition from Galatea Atredides. She sat primly—as befitted her station—and when angry voices were raised in protest to helping the Venturians, stood slowly, drawing the eyes of each woman there.

"As you know," she said, "I have reason to be grateful for the assistance of Lord Konan Krull, Lord High Commander of the Venturian Forces. I did not ask for his help when my niece Jeinna was taken. He offered and I accepted. When her..." Queen Mona stopped, momentarily overcome with grief, "...when her body was returned to us, I sent word to Lord Krull to relieve him of his vow to find and kill the men who took Jeinna." She looked around her, meeting every Councilwoman's eye. "Nevertheless, he continued on to Nebul—at the risk of his own life—found the men and avenged my family."

"Such is the way of a man with six daughters of his own," Galatea Atredides commented.

"True, and Konan Krull is an honorable man who strives to do the right thing," Queen Mona agreed.

"And because of his boon to you, we are to risk our warrioresses?" Flavia Pantasriste, the Abbess of Education, smirked.

"What he did for Mona, he did for us," Queen Deianeira, the defense queen of the Amazeen said. "It could just have well been one of ours those Nebullian pigs murdered. We all have kin at the Abbey."

"Does Lady Isabell know you slept with her husband, Queen Mona?" Flavia asked.

"For shame, Flavia!" Queen Antianeira, the Amazeen domestic queen said, her eyes wide. "We do not bring personalities to the Council of Elders!"

There was low rumbling among those gathered, but none turned their eyes to Queen Mona. Flavia shrugged, crossed her legs and arms, and looked away. Her manner was of one being bored at the proceedings.

Queen Mona could feel the stare of her young daughter scalding her but refused to look down at Lilit. It was bad enough that the child knew of that ill-favored affair of so long ago. To have her be a witness to her mother's shame before the assemblage of the Council brought fresh pain to the Queen's heart.

"If my vote counts here," Queen Mona said, her head high, "I vote we help the Venturians." With that, she sat down again, her hands folded gracefully in her lap.

"Your vote most assuredly does count here," Queen Antianeira stated. "We must, however, have a majority. Do we call for the vote now or shall we discuss this matter further?"

"I say let us vote and be done with it," Flavia snapped. "I vote no."

"I vote no, as well," Okypous, one of the other Councilwomen — the Abbess of Healing and Flavia's only friend — piped up.

"Well, I vote to help Lord Krull," Queen Deianeira responded.

"Since I brought this matter before the Council, I vote to help," Galatea said.

Kynthia was there — not as a member of the Council — but as an observer. She knew it would be necessary to have at least seven of the thirteen Councilwomen vote in agreement in order for the motion to carry to help Ventura. Five of the Councilwomen were Amazeens, five were Daughters of the Night and two — Galatea and Celadina, from the Daughters of the Multitude. The remaining member — and the one whose vote would break a tie—was the Mother Superior of the Abbey at Marpesia.

"Lord Krull has been a stalwart ally over the years. He has never made war on us as the Akkadian once did," Lysippe Iphito remarked. "I vote to help the Venturians."

"It is to our advantage to be rid of Abalam Robeus and have his daughter take the throne. Though she is not of our assemblage, she is a Daughter, I am told," Queen Antianeira said.

"She is a Daughter of the Multitude, aye," Galatea offered. "Her practice of the arts must be kept secret for her sire is a mad dog, as we all know, and would surely put her to the stake if he felt like it."

"I vote yes," Queen Antianeira said.

"Six votes to two," Celadina, Kynthia's sister announced, "for my vote is to help."

"I vote no," Eurybe, Abbess of Agriculture put in. "I've no love for the Venturians any more than the Akkadians and Pleiadesians. What help have any of them ever given us when there was famine or drought?"

"Lord Krull sent water wagons to Bandar when there was a drought four years ago," Queen Mona said softly. "And as I remember, he also sent flour and grains to you a year before that."

"Because you lay with him," Flavia spat.

"That is enough!" Queen Antianeira shouted. "I will have no more of your wicked tongue. If you can not be civil in this assembly, take yourself from it!"

"I vote no, as well," another Councilwoman spoke up. "I have no beef with Krull but I do not like sending our women to a war that is not of our making."

"Six to four, then," Flavia's friend Okypous said smugly. She turned to the woman beside her. "What say you, Harmothoe?"

"I vote no," the Abbess of Womanly Arts replied.

"Six to five," Okypous said. "That leaves Antiopeia and the Mother Superior."

"I vote no," Antiopeia, the Abbess of Sporting said.

"We have a tie," Queen Antianeira said with a sigh. "Mother Superior, how do you vote?"

Mother Tecmessa swept her gaze around the room. She studied Galatea, Kynthia then finally Queen Mona. Known for her impartiality and her wisdom, she had been the Mother Superior at the Abbey for over thirty years. Each of the women seated on the Council of Elders had studied their letters under Tecmessa and she knew them all well.

The Councilwomen and those who had been allowed to sit in on the discussion and vote locked their gazes on Mother Tecmessa, and waited breathlessly for her to cast the deciding vote.

"Krull," Mother Tecmessa finally said, "has proven himself a friend to both the Amazeen and the Daughters of the Night. What—if anything—he has done for the Multitude remains to be seen, but should not enter into the decision here. As we have been reminded, it is to our advantage to be rid of Abalam Robeus. He is an evil man who preys on young children and for that alone, he should be cast into the lowest depths of the Abyss."

The women nodded and voiced their agreement to that statement.

"To turn aside when we are asked to help a man who has gone out of his way to help us, who, in fact, risked his life to avenge the brutal death of one of our own, would make us no better than the thieving Pleiades or the arrogant Akkadians. Therefore, my vote is yes."

Applause broke out among those who voted and those who could not but were behind the plan.

"But…" Mother Tecmessa said, holding up her hand for silence. "If the Lord High Commander of the Venturian Forces and his Captain of the Guard wish our help, they must come and ask for it. They must come alone — without escort — to prove they trust us if we are to trust them. Only then will we agree to ride beside them — not behind them — into battle."

Galatea turned and looked at Kynthia. "Will they do it?"

Kynthia shrugged. "I don't know. I would think so, but I will have to ask Leksi." On impulse, she stood up. "If," she said, drawing all eyes to her. "If they agree to come, will their safety be guaranteed?" She turned her stare to Flavia.

"Why? Are the little boy soldiers afraid of us?" Flavia asked with a chuckle. "They should be. I've the right eye and thumb of many a man pickled in brine and lined up neatly on a shelf over my desk."

A few of those gathered laughed at the boast, but Queen Antianeira had had enough and stood up, her arm straight out in front of her, finger pointing. "Leave this room, Flavia Pantasriste. We have endured enough of your venom and spite for one evening!"

Flavia shot to her feet, swept her gown aside and flounced from the room, Okypous like a little puppy following a few steps behind.

"You'd better watch that one, Kynni," Celadina whispered. "I don't trust her or that smarmy little toad who hopped away behind her."

"Will the warriors' safety be guaranteed?" Kynthia asked again.

"No woman's hand will be lifted against them," Queen Antianeira vowed. "This I swear for all the Amazeen."

* * * * *

Flavia cursed viciously as she swept into her quarters. So angry was she, she forgot Okypous was behind her and slammed the door in the other woman's surprised face. A timid knock on the door brought instantaneous fury to the face of the Abbess of Education and when she threw the door open, was only mildly appeased to find her only friend and supporter standing there.

"Well, don't just hover there like a timid hummingbird, Okypous. Come in!" Flavia ordered.

"If this is a bad time, Lady Flavia—"

"What is the name of that cousin of yours in Nebul?" Flavia interrupted.

"Phoebe?"

"No, fool!" Flavia snarled. "The male!"

"Oh," Okypous said, her face brightening. "You mean Sorath."

"Aye," Flavia said, narrowing her eyes. "That was the bastard's name. He is something in the Pleiadesian government, is he not?"

"I believe he is the Chief of the Secret Police," was the reply.

Flavia smiled nastily. "Think you he might be interested to know there is a plan afoot to invade his country?"

Okypous frowned. "We would let him know our warrioresses are coming?" she asked, her voice strained. "Would that not be a treasonous thing to do?"

"Of course not, you dolt!" Flavia shouted, and struck the other woman a vicious blow. "Our women will never leave Amazeen's borders if I have anything to say about it!"

Staggered by the brutal slap, Okypous stood with her palm pressed to the stinging pain. She was shivering and dared ask nothing more for fear Flavia would attack her again.

"I want you to get a message to your cousin and use that special code you once told me about. We don't want anyone to be able to decipher the missive should someone intercept the messenger. We do *not* want anyone to know what we are about," Flavia was saying as she paced back and forth, her hands clasped behind her back. "Tell your cousin, Konan Krull and Leksi Helios will be making a trek to Amazeen within the next few days. Since they will be coming across our southwestern border from Tasjorn, he can have a troop lying in wait to capture them on the Qabala side."

"Ah," Okypous said, and flinched as Flavia turned to glare at her.

"Tell him under no circumstances is he to allow the Venturians to cross over to Amazeen land. They must be taken before entering our lands. Stress that to him. The Qabalans won't interfere, cowards that they are, so there should be no worry there."

A thought crossed Okypous' mind and she opened her mouth to speak it, but was terrified of Flavia's reaction. Instead, she clamped her lips shut and looked down at the floor.

"What?" Flavia demanded. "You have something to say?"

Her shoulders hunched in anticipation of a blow, Okypous asked what should happen if the Pleiadesians should slay the Venturians. Would not the Council of Elders find out about it and lay the blame on her and Flavia?

"Of course those bloodthirsty bastards won't kill the great Lord High Commander, you fucking idiot! Nor would they murder Helios," Flavia said. "Abalam would like nothing better than to have those two handsome brutes in his dungeon. Can you imagine the exquisite pain he will put them through?"

Unease rode Okypous' shoulders. She gnawed on her lip until a bead of blood oozed over the thin surface. She stood watching Flavia pacing, talking all manner of wildness as she walked. Though she knew she should report this scheme of Flavia's, she knew she would not. To do so would be to court certain death.

"Go," Flavia ordered, taking hold of Okypous' arm in a punishing grip and propelling her to the door. "Send word now to your cousin, and make sure whomever you send does not return to report where she went!"

Chapter Nine

Kynthia was waiting at the stream. The sun had set but a few moments before and the onset of autumn was in the air. She hovered in her cloak, wrapping it around her as though she were cold. In truth, she was not. Reapers rarely felt the cold for their body temperatures are much higher than a normal person's. What she was feeling was nervousness and anticipation and as she drew the rough material of her light cloak up to her nose—only her eyes peeked out beneath the voluminous hood—she shifted from foot to foot.

A low growl came from Kirkor, and the white wolf got up from where it laid in a patch of grass and turned to the east.

"Is it him?"

The wolf looked back at her and seemed to grin.

"Go find your lady then," she commanded. "I want no voyeurs about when I get my hands on the warrior."

Kirkor shook his body, his tail whipping from side-to-side then he loped away, looking back once before disappearing in the forest beyond the stream.

Throwing aside her cloak, Kynthia smoothed the fabric of her gown over her thighs—she adjusted the bodice, tugging the short sleeves into place. Not the type of clothing she normally wore, she felt uncomfortable in the garment but beneath it, her legs were bare—free of stocking or boots. Likewise, she wore no banding about her breasts. She wanted no impediments to the warrior's touch. The gown itself was of poor quality and she did not mind if it got ripped. In Aeolus' saddlebags, there was a blouse and pair of breeches for later use.

Along with that wondrous portion of the warrior's anatomy she could not stop thinking about.

"You are turning into a slut, Kynthia," she mumbled to herself.

The neighing of a horse drew her attention and she squinted in that direction. Sniffing the air, her keen sense of smell caught Leksi Helios' scent and her womb quickened. When the warrior came into view, she felt giddy with lust.

He was out of the saddle and running toward her, his strong arms opened wide. She flew to him, jumping into his arms, her legs wrapped around his waist and as their mouths locked upon one another, he swung her around and around.

The kiss was deep, their tongues dueling. Her breasts were pressed tightly to his hard chest and she could feel his stony erection pressing against her belly. He staggered a bit when he stopped spinning them around then dropped to his knees with a grunt muffled by her mouth.

His momentum carried her to her back and he was fumbling at the skirt to her gown, shoving it aside so he could get his hand between her legs. The moment his palm touched the core of her, Kynthia came, her vaginal muscles tightening in quick little spasms that made her squeal with delight. She tore her mouth free of his and squealed again—a high-pitched tone of pure satiation.

"It would seem you missed me, wench," he teased.

She made no reply but released his hips from her tight embrace and twisted her body, flipping over so their positions were reversed. She was above him, sitting upon his thighs, the skirt of her gown bunched around her own.

"That's twice you have pleasured me, warrior, and I've yet to return the favor," she said in a husky voice.

Leksi started to speak but her hands were on the clasp of his breeches, her fingers flying through the buttons. He gulped as she slipped her hand inside the fly and drew out his cock. The warmth of her hand was so intense he sighed with the sheer pleasure of it.

She stroked that long, erect tool and ran her fingertip over the slit in the tip, allowing her fingernail to delve gently inside.

"Wench!" Leksi gasped.

"Lay still, warrior and let me be about my business," she said.

She leaned down and blew her hot breath across the head. It was all Leksi could do not to grab her, but he laid immobile, his blood beginning to quicken and his body trembling slightly.

Trying to remember all her aunt had imparted to her during their ride back from the Amazeen keep, Kynthia lightly gripped his weapon with one hand while she stroked its length with her other. She paid close attention to the underside of the head.

"Kynthia, I am—"

"Hush!" she ordered, and with one lithe movement was on her knees at his feet, tugging off his boots.

Leksi raised his head and watched as she drew off first one boot then the other, stripped him of his stockings then returned to his breeches. With a wicked gleam in her eyes, she tugged at the waistband and began drawing the breeches off, aided by the warrior lifting his hips to accommodate her.

Next, she made quick work of his shirt, ripping the buttons apart. He laughed and when she spread his arms up above his head, accommodated her further by spreading his legs. What she did next made him draw in a quick, shocked breath.

She turned so that her backside was to him and used her feet to anchor his wrists to the ground. Firmly gripping his thighs to keep them spread, she lowered her head and took his erect member into her mouth.

"Wench!" he warned, sucking in another stunned breath.

Kynthia smiled as she withdrew her intimate embrace and giggled when she heard his groan of frustration. Once more, she gripped his penis, bent her head and, pushing his penis down, licked him slowly from just above his anus all the way across his balls and then to the tip of his cock. As she felt him stiffen beneath her, she reached up with one hand, spread apart the slit in his penis with her fingers, and then used the tip of her tongue to flick mercilessly at the head.

"Shit!" Leksi warned, bucking beneath her.

Before he could come, she took him into her mouth and drew hard on that straining shaft, her lips pressed tightly. With a heavy grunt, he came, his hands clawing at her ankles. One long shudder gripped him, he bellowed his release, and then he lay limp beneath her, his head tilted to one side.

Her aunt had told Kynthia she might not like the taste of a man's love juice or the feel of it in her mouth but that it was a natural way to pleasure your lover. To Kynthia, the taste wasn't all that bad so she swallowed it.

"Wench?" he questioned.

She turned around, wiping her lips with the heel of her palm. "Aye, warrior?" she returned.

"The next time, I will be atop you and inside you," he said softly.

"Well, I should hope so," she said, stretching out beside him.

He took her into his arms and nuzzled his face against her neck. She smelled faintly of lemons and he drew in a deep breath, enjoying the scent.

She twirled a strand of his chest hair around her finger then ran her hand over the crisp wiriness of that broad expanse. She liked the feel of his hard muscles and the ridges of his hard paps. Using her palm, she massaged those manly nipples and idly plucked at them with her fingertips.

"If you keep that up, a situation might arise, wench," he warned.

"Like I said — I hope so," she told him.

Smoothing her hand down his flat belly, her palm gliding over ridges of striated muscle, she slid her fingers into the wiry curls at the juncture of his thighs, plucking at them lightly.

"Did your aunt give you a lesson or two since last we met?" he asked.

"I believe something was mentioned," she replied.

"That woman is a veritable font of knowledge," he said with a grin. "Her Ocnus taught her well."

Kynthia craned her head and looked up at him. "What makes you think it was Ocnus who taught her and not the other way around?" she teased.

Leksi smiled and closed his eyes, enjoying the lassitude that was settling over him. His free hand was traveling up and down her bare arm and he marveled at how soft her skin was.

"I should discuss a bit of business with you," she said, sensing he was on the verge of falling asleep.

"I would rather not," he said.

"Nevertheless, it is important."

The warrior sighed. "All right, wench. What?"

"The Council of Elders has agreed to help you with the problem but there is a catch."

Leksi opened his eyes. "What kind of catch?" he asked, frowning.

"They wish for you and Lord Krull to come to them and put your petition before the assemblage." When he tensed and a low growl came from him, she pushed herself up on one elbow. "Your safety has been guaranteed and it is simply a matter of courtesy that they wish you to journey to Amazeen."

"Courtesy," he repeated.

"Aye. There is much admiration of you and Lord Krull in Amazeen, but this is a request you should not dismiss."

Leksi looked her in the eye. "I will have to run it by Lord Krull. He has no great love of the warrioresses."

"No, but he did help them during both the famine and the drought."

"Aye, so they owe him."

Kynthia sighed. "And will repay him. It is strictly a matter of courtesy on his part." She began toying with his shaft.

Leksi sighed. "All right. I'll add my recommendation that we go to Amazeen."

"Good," she said, and began paying closer attention to his burgeoning member.

The warrior drew in a long, deep breath and as her fingers slid down his length, felt the stirrings of passion once more. He lay there until her delicate ministrations had him hard as a rock then very gently turned her to her back.

"I will repay you in kind for earlier, milady, but for now, I will claim you as mine once and for all," he said, looking down into her eyes.

Very gently and slowly, he sat up and held his hand out to her. When she was up, he reached out with trembling fingers and unbuttoned her bodice, helping her out of it, careful not to touch the glorious breasts that taunted him. With her help, he eased the gown from her long legs and drew in a ragged breath as the scent of her filled his nostrils. He knelt there for a moment, taking in her beauty, deliberately avoiding looking at her crotch for just the thought of those wiry curls made his mouth water and his palms itch to caress them.

"Lie down, my love," he said in a husky voice and when she was once more lying on her back, he stretched out beside her.

Kynthia stiffened as he nudged her legs apart but he did no more than lie atop her, his sword pressing against her crotch, his cheek pillowed upon her chest. As she had toyed with his nipples, so did he toy with hers and when she squirmed beneath his weight, lifted up only enough to position himself at the entrance of her vagina.

"It will be tight and perhaps a bit uncomfortable for me to enter you, my love, but I will be as gentle as I know how to be."

She relaxed and when the tip of him pushed gently inside her, she closed her eyes, giving herself up to whatever he did.

"Look at me, Kynni," he whispered.

Her eyes fluttered open and he could see the wound still deep in their gray depths. Not for the first time he wished he had the Basarabian demon that had raped her in his clutches.

"Your cunt will ooze around me when I am fully seated. There will be less friction. Just relax and trust me."

With firm, steady pressure, he slid carefully inside her then lay still, for he could sense her discomfort and he wanted to wait until she was fully moist before he began to thrust.

Kynthia marveled at how he filled her. Though she was nervous, afraid he would unintentionally hurt her, it was thrilling to have him impaling her.

Very slowly, he withdrew just a bit then settled back to near the limit of his length. He was not a boastful man but he knew himself to be larger than the average man, though not nearly as well hung as Konan Krull.

"How would you know how that warrior's equipment looks?" she asked in a curious tone.

At first Leksi wondered how she had intercepted his thoughts then remembered that Reapers had that astonishing ability. He laughed. "Men surreptitiously spy on one another when they are at bath or the like. We tend to compare our equipment, as you call it."

"Like when you're pissing you compare sizes?"

"No!" he said, shock flaring his eyes. "That's considered bad manners, wench."

"Oh," she said. "And Lord Krull is bigger than you?" She asked it in a voice that hinted such a thing was doubtful.

"Not that you are ever going to find out," he said firmly, "but, aye. He is much larger than I."

"And does his lady-wife find that painful?"

"By all accounts, Lady Isabell finds it much to her liking. They have six children."

"I like the length of you. Though he hurt me, Minos had the prick the size of a worm's." She snorted. "Now, he's worm meat!"

Leksi chuckled and as he did, his cock wriggled inside her and before he could still the movement, his lady had wrapped her legs around his hips, anchoring him as deeply inside her as he could get.

"I'm tired of this tenderness, warrior," she said through clenched teeth. "Claim me, now!"

Her heel was dug between the cheeks of his ass and the sensation prodded him even more than her words. Throwing caution to the winds, he began pumping inside and was soon so caught up in the rhythm and the superb pleasure squeezing his flesh, he was slamming against her.

There had been a moment or two of pain but Kynthia knew that had to be. That pain was soon taken over with the most delicious of sensations rippling through her body. She clung to her lover and lifted her hips up to meet his short, shallow strokes, wishing he'd go deeper.

Leksi felt the first clenches of her vaginal muscles around the tip of his cock and lengthened his stroke. As soon as he felt her straining against him, he pushed deep and held.

The pleasure was so intense, so completely enthralling, Kynthia arched her head back and screamed with her release. Her lover echoed her cry for he jerked inside her and pumped like mad two or three times before stilling then collapsing atop her, shuddering.

She wrapped her arms around him and licked a droplet of sweat from his shoulder. At last, she was his and he was hers.

"I love you, Leksi Helios," she whispered.

"And I you, Kynthia Ancaeus," he replied.

Somewhere off in the distance, a wolf howled and Kynthia sighed contentedly. Kirkor had serviced his mate, too, and just wanted his human friend to know.

Chapter Ten

Where Qabala met Ventura was a mere spit of ground no more than a few hundred feet long and ten feet broad at its widest point. On a map, it looked to be a crooked finger with Ventura the fist of the hand and Qabala the finger, the Rysalian Gulf on one side and the Sea of Aziz on the other. In order to journey from Ventura to the Amazeen lands, a traveler had to pass over that finger of land. At the tip, Qabala spread out again for about a mile before joining with Amazeen to the West. There at the tip, the land slanted downward then up at a fairly good incline so that one trekked through a valley that had once been part of the Sea of Aziz. With large boulders and sheer cliffs to either side of the well-traveled roadway, there was always a chance of being set upon by thieves. Though there had never been an incident in which someone traveling that spit of land known as the Bridge of Naji had been robbed, experienced travelers took into consideration the lay of the land and kept a close watch on their surroundings.

Lord Krull and Leksi were no different. Each was diligent in surveying the area around them as they entered the Valley of Kaseeb. Each rode with his hand upon the dagger at his side, the sword sheathed on his back well oiled for ease of drawing and honed to razor thinness.

"I've a prickling sensation in my nuts," Krull said softly.

"I'm uneasy, as well," Leksi replied.

There was something in the air, and by rights that should not be, for they were on Qabalan land and the Qabalans were a neutral people. First to flee a fight if they could not reason with an enemy, the people of Qabala were known cowards.

"Do you think we're riding into a trap?" Leksi asked.

"I think we're being watched, if nothing else," his commander answered. He squinted, thinking he had seen a flash of light off to his right.

"Do you hear that?" Leksi asked.

"I don't hear anything," Krull said.

"Neither do I and I find that strange, don't you?"

Krull pulled on his mount's reins and bent over the steed's neck, patting the point of its shoulder as though something ailed the beast. Instead, he was listening attentively but his Captain was right—there was nothing to hear and that in itself was out of the ordinary.

"There should be sea bird calls along the coast if nothing else," Leksi said.

"And the thump of mining machines from the quarry at Yasar," Krull reasoned. "That's less than two miles east of us." He looked up at the sky. "It's too early for them to have knocked off for lunch and to my knowledge there was no Qabalan holiday declared." He straightened up in the saddle.

"Something isn't right."

"I agree."

"Perhaps we should turn around."

Krull took the water skin from his saddle horn and uncorked it. He took a long pull on the tepid liquid, his keen eyes sawing back and forth across the vista before them. When he lowered the water skin, he offered Leksi a drink.

"Twenty degrees to your left," the Lord High Commander stated. "We've got company over there."

Leksi took the water skin, drank, swished the water around in his mouth, and then turned his head to spit out the water. As he did, he caught sight of the horsemen partially hidden behind a cliff. "I see them," he said, handing the water skin back to Krull.

"We'll be going up either way we run," Krull said, "but the trek back is the steeper path. I don't see we have a choice."

"Chances are there are more riders up there behind those boulders," Leksi commented.

"I'd stake my commission on it," Krull agreed.

"What do you suggest?"

Before Krull could answer, a bloodthirsty yell came from behind them and the warriors turned to see a group of at least a dozen men spurring their mounts down the incline over which Krull and Leksi had just passed. Another yell signaled the advance of riders coming from behind the boulders. Outnumbered ten to one, the warriors glanced at one another.

"Go with the Wind, Leksi," Krull said, reaching up to draw his sword.

"I will look for you in Paradise, milord."

Kicking their horses into action, the warriors engaged their enemies head on, the flash of their blades blindingly fast in the late morning sun. The skirl of metal sliding along metal, sword edge meeting sword edge with a deadly tattoo and with sparks flying, echoed off the high walls of the valley. The sounds of men grunting, cursing, shouting orders drowned out the excited whinny of the horses and the occasional cry of the wounded.

Krull was a powerful warrior with no compassion for his enemies lurking within his robust breast. He fought viciously, brutally with a dogged determination to kill as many men as his sword could pierce. His athletic prowess was known far and wide, and those foolish enough to take him on knew they had no chance to engage him fairly in battle. Underhanded tricks would have to be the order of the day. While one attacker met the Lord High Commander's sword blade-on, another used a slingshot to fling small, sharp rocks at Krull's back and shoulders, his legs and arms. The cowardly attack was more annoying than painful although Krull's concentration was badly affected as his frustration and temper rose. Twice he was unable to stop himself from turning his head around when a particularly sharp rock struck his flesh and because of that, he had two nasty cuts along his left forearm.

"Take them alive!" had been the cry as the Nebullian warriors began their attack and knowing this, both Krull and Leksi were determined to take as many of their enemies down before they fell beneath their enemies' onslaught.

Leksi was fairing no better than his Commander, and was bleeding profusely from several nasty cuts on his arms. The loss of blood was weakening him rapidly and he was woozy. He stumbled backward, lost his footing, and fell to the ground, a sword point to his throat.

"Beg quarter, Pretty One," his attacker said with a grin, and dug the point of his weapon into the hollow of the warrior's neck until a trickle of blood eased down Leksi's throat. "It would be a shame to close those sweet little eyes forever."

"Go fuck yourself," Leksi seethed between clenched teeth. Had he been able to, he would have swept his weapon up into the gut of the man hovering over him but another attacker was standing on Leksi's arm, grinding the sole of his boot against the fallen warrior's wrist.

Leksi's opponent threw back his head and laughed. He removed his sword from the younger man's throat and saluted him. "You are a brave — if foolish — young man." He nodded to the man standing on Leksi's wrist. "Get him up."

Krull was still fighting but there were five men circling him, each reaching out to nick the warrior's arms and back. His shirt was bloody and he was staggering as he lashed out, panting in between curses. Tripping over a foot stuck out to bring him down, he was so winded and weak from his own blood loss, he had no energy left to stop his enemies from taking hold of him.

It was a one-sided fight that saw only four attackers dead and as many wounded by the time it was over. Sweaty and defeated, Krull and Leksi were driven to their knees, their arms drawn behind them with heavy shackles that pulled brutally at their shoulders.

The burly man in charge of the attackers had not engaged in the battle. He had been watching from the sidelines but now strode arrogantly to Leksi and reached down to grip the young man's chin and jerk his head back. "You're right, Khaliq. He is a pretty boy," the man chortled. "The king will have a fine time with him!"

"Go to hell," Leksi snarled, and tried to pull his face free of the man's brutal hold.

"You'll squeal like a pig when he rams it into you, boy. He likes to hear them squeal."

Konan Krull made no threats as he was jerked to his feet. It was useless to speak to the troopers who had ridden down on them. They were merely following orders and had no say in the final outcome of the attack. Though he was itching to know who had told the Nebullians their plans, he knew he'd get nothing out of the bastard in charge.

"So you are the all-powerful Krull," the one in charge said, snorting. He hawked up a wad of phlegm and spat it at Krull's feet. "You don't look like much to me."

"Looks can be deceiving," Krull said, his eyes steady on the man.

The leader's eyes fluttered and he stepped closer, his offensive body odor far more lethal than the clumsy blade he had wielded during the attack.

"We'll see how cocky you are when King Abalam is finished coring you, Lord Krull. I don't think you'll be quite so arrogant then."

Leksi was pulled up and shoved toward his horse. Before he could curse the man who had slapped him in the middle of his back, another had reached out to grab him between the legs. Eyes wide, lips drawn back from his teeth, Leksi lashed out with his foot and caught the abuser in the balls, planting his boot firmly and with savagery in the other man's crotch.

A yowl of agony ripped out of the man's throat and he fell to the ground, his hands wrapped protectively around his wounded parts. Rolling back and forth and groaning in pain, he was ignored as another man lifted Leksi and plopped him down in the saddle.

"You are quick, boy," the leader scoffed, "but when the king is finished with you, you'll be down on your knees sucking Wafid's cock for having done that to him! I can tell you now he's going to shove it down your pretty little throat until you choke!"

The other men laughed and as Krull was lifted to his mount and his ankles—as were Leksi's—lashed together beneath the belly of the horse, the leader went over to see to the injured man.

"Get up, Wafid," the leader ordered, nudging the moaning man with the toe of his boot. "You'll have your time with the Pretty One."

"I w-will c-cut off his b-balls!" Wafid vowed as he struggled to stand.

"I'm sure the king will gather you an audience for that," the leader conceded.

Leksi had a black eye and several shallows cut along his forearm, a few scrapes and bruises but nothing major. Krull was suffering from a bitch of a headache caused by the blunt end of an attacker's sword to back of the Lord High Commander's neck, felling him from his mount. Along with the various shallow cuts on his arms, there was also a gash on his cheek from when he'd fallen to the rocky ground. Other than those injuries, the warriors were pestered more by wounded pride than anything else. Both were furious that they had allowed themselves to be captured, and neither had any illusions about what awaited them at Abalam's keep.

* * * * *

Okypous was on her hands and knees before Queen Antianeira. The stout woman's ugly face was screwed into a mask of terror and tears flowed copiously down her cheeks. Her hands were clenched under her chin, her voice a mere shriek of sound as she rocked on her knees and begged forgiveness for her sins, her babbling words accented with hiccups of hysteria.

"What sin is she babbling about?" Queen Deianeira demanded.

"I have no idea," Queen Antianeira replied. "Get the hell up, woman. It is unseemly for you to be wallowing around like that!"

Okypous shot to her feet, but was so afraid of her Queens she could do little more than whimper. Still bobbing back and forth, she began shaking her head, flinging her unbound hair this way and that.

"What in the hell is wrong with her?" Queen Deianeira asked. "Where is Flavia?"

"At the Abbey," her twin sister answered. She stepped down from her throne, drew back her hand, and slapped Okypous as hard as she could, staggering the heavier woman.

Eyes flared wide, Okypous dropped to her knees once more and wrapped her arms around Antianeira's legs. "Forgive me, Majesty!" she pleaded. "Forgive me!"

"For what?" Antianeira shouted.

"I did not want to do it, but Flavia would have killed me. I…"

Queen Deianeira was beside the distraught woman in a flash and hunkered down beside her. She grabbed a handful of Okypous' hair and dragged her head back. "What did you do?"

"I s-sent a message to my cousin," Okypous stuttered, and a bubble of snot burst from her nose.

In disgust, Queen Deianeira shoved the woman away and got to her feet, her lips twisted with repulsion.

"Sent what cousin a message?"

"Sorath Nergal," Okypous confessed.

The twin sisters exchanged a look. "The Chief of the Secret Police in Nebul?"

"Aye," Okypous whined. She covered her face with her hands. "I am so sorry, so very sorry. Forgive me!"

"Once more you have allowed that bitch Flavia to lead you into mischief," Queen Antianeira said. "Why do I suspect this is real trouble you've gotten yourself into this time?"

"I did not want to do it, Your Majesty," Okypous moaned. "I knew it was wrong."

"What did you tell your cousin, whore?"

"The plan," Okypous whimpered. "Oh, Alluvia! I beg forgiveness!"

Antianeira and Deianeira looked at one another. "The Pleiadesians know Krull is coming," Deianeira said.

"He should have been here by now. The sun has only an hour left in the sky," Antianeira remarked.

"And he would have been unless there was an unwelcoming party sent out to snare him."

The sisters turned their furious eyes to Okypous. "This was Flavia's doing?" Antianeira wanted clarified.

"Aye," Okypous moaned, the word drawn out.

"Why?" the Domestic Queen demanded. "She never does anything without a personal motivation. What is in it for her?"

"I don't know, Majesty. She didn't explain her reasons to me."

"This isn't a case of trying to thwart us," Antianeira said. "There's more to it."

Queen Deianeira looked to one of the two Amazeen guards stationed at the door to the throne room. "Gather a squad and go after Flavia. Bring that treasonous bitch back in chains but make sure she is unharmed. I want the pleasure of chopping off her head myself when this is done!"

The guard had snapped to attention the moment her Queen's eyes fell on her. With a slap of her balled fist to her heart, she took a step back, pivoted on the toe of her boot and spun around, making haste to do as she was bid.

"And you," Deianeira said, pointing at the remaining guard, "send a fast rider to Galatea's villa and alert her niece to what has happened. She will want to go after her lover."

"And wind up in the harems of Abalam's vile Tribunal?" her sister challenged.

"Nay, not that one. She'll know what she should do."

"Do we ride against the Pleiadesians along with her?"

"No. We are outnumbered unless we have the Venturians and the Hell Hags with us. Go, sound the alarm. I will gather my warrioresses together and send messengers to Tasjorn and Bandar. It is time we put an end to Abalam Robeus once and for all!"

"What about the Qabalans?"

Queen Deianeira's face showed her disdain. "They wish to remain neutral? Let them. When we put Clea on the throne of Pleiades, we'll make her Regent of Qabala, as well. The Qabalan king is a fool at best. He won't gainsay us!"

Chapter Eleven

Kynthia was not at her aunt's villa when the messenger arrived, her lathered pony heaving for air.

"She's gone after him, and her sisters and I are preparing to follow," Galatea informed the messenger. "I also sent word to Queen Mona."

"My Queen will wish to know who told you of this," the messenger said.

"No one needed to. Kynthia knew the moment her man was taken," Galatea said. "She has powers."

Never one to question the gifts of the gods, the messenger nodded, wished Galatea and her nieces a safe journey with the Wind, and then turned her horse to race back to Amazeen where she hoped to join those headed into battle.

"I've never seen Kynthia so angry," Haidee said as she came out of the keep, her quiver of arrows lashed securely to her back.

"I pray she calms down before she reaches Nebul," Galatea replied. "It will be full night by then and not a one of those barbarians will survive a meeting with our Reaper."

"And that's a bad thing?" Erinyes sneered. "Let her drain every last heathen one of them!"

Galatea rolled her eyes. "Have you no concept of what stealth battle is all about, Erinyes? Have you learned nothing I have taught you?"

"You can draw more flies with honey than vinegar," Celadina quipped as she strapped her dagger to her waist and adjusted the sheath. "Our sister will need to be calm and levelheaded if she is to get inside that dungeon and find her man."

"Aye," Ophelia agreed. "Going in there in a frenzy will only get her hurt." She looked at her aunt. "Or worse."

"It will take a sharp blade across the neck to stop Kynthia," Galatea said. "Wounded, she will be more vicious than her enemies. That is why I say she must be calm. She can walk right by the guards if she but puts those Reaper powers of hers to work."

* * * * *

Cainer Cree felt the same way. He was sending messages to Kynthia as she rode hell-bent for leather along the coast road to Pleiades. He was speaking softly to her, stressing each word, cautioning her to think before she acted.

"They have my mate!" she shouted, the wind whipping her hair as her steed galloped across the sand.

Aye, but he is alive still. Think, Kynthia. Do not act rashly. You will be no good to him otherwise.

Knowing she had a superior warrior instructing her, Kynthia silently agreed to temper her fury. A part of her was livid with rage while another shrank at what might be happening to Leksi.

You would feel it if he were being hurt, the Reaper reminded her. *Concentrate on him, listen to his thoughts. You'll find him quicker that way.*

Kynthia was bent low over her mount's neck, her heels drumming into the beast's straining side, urging it to a faster speed. Her hands gripped the reins so tightly the leather was cutting into her palms.

You have never used the ability to make others overlook you, wench. Listen to me and learn how it is done.

"Why do I...?"

How else will you get into the dungeon to free your lover? the Reaper snarled. *Listen to what I say!*

And so she listened, and when the lights of Abalam's keep could be seen glittering in the distance, she turned her mind from Cree's words to try to find Leksi in the teeming mass that was Nebul.

"I can't hear him!" she cried, tears filling her eyes.

I can, the Reaper said calmly. *You are not trying hard enough, wench.*

"How can you hear him?"

Because you took a part of him inside you. You tasted that one droplet of blood upon his cut cheek therefore you have a portion of his DNA and the parasite can smell it. It sought him out, homing in on his position and sent word to the Queen. It is through her that I can hear him.

Cainer did not tell her he was blocking Kynthia's "hearing" of her lover's thoughts, for within the last few moments the man had begun screaming in pain. The Reaper knew in order for her to act rationally, she had to stay calm and cold, and detached. If she knew the man she loved was being tortured, she would get herself caught.

He is in the deepest section of the dungeon, wench, the Reaper told her. *Here is how to find him.*

Kynthia paid close attention to Cree, though she worried that she could not hear Leksi's thoughts. She knew the Reaper was pulling the directions of how to reach her lover's cell from Leksi's memories of being taken to that vile place. If Cree could hear him, she knew he was still alive.

By the time you free your man, the Amazeen and Daughters will be at the gates. There will be a ruckus unlike anything you've ever heard but pay no attention to it. You will need to go ahead and make Helios One with the Blood. Do you understand?

"How?" she shouted. "You said the beastess would not allow me to —"

Konan Krull is with Helios. He will have to be the one to harvest the fledgling. He won't understand, wench. You will need to make him do as you bid. Is that clear? Don't give him a chance to balk. Time will be of the essence.

Though it was the last thing she could imagine settling in her mind, her own impregnation of the Reaper's nestling washed over Kynthia's mind. She could see the blade in Galatea's hand. She winced at the remembered feel of the incision that her aunt had opened on her back. She could hear her aunt's hiss of disgust as she plucked the fledgling from its jar and dropped it to Kynthia's back. The memory of the ungodly pain seared Kynthia's brain and took every other worry from her thoughts.

"Stop it, Cree!" she bellowed. "I remember well what it felt like!"

Never forget it, he said softly, *for it is the very life of you.*

Just as she had been forced to gain her aunt's cooperation in helping her to become One with the Blood, she knew she'd have just as much trouble convincing Lord Krull that it had to be done.

But why?

Aye, Leksi had mentioned in passing that he would not be averse to becoming a Reaper but why was Cainer Cree insisting on it?

How close are you to the gates of the keep?

The intrusion of the Reaper's thoughts broke into Kynthia's.

"Just a few hundred yards," she replied.

The Reaper knew he had to stop her wondering about why she needed to turn Helios. Once she was inside the dungeon and got a look at his battered and broken body, she would know.

Do as I told you. Think of the fog that drifts down through the mountains. Imagine it thick and milky white, so thick it is nearly impossible to walk through. Cloak yourself and your steed in that fog, wench. Let it drown out all sound of your passing. And when you dismount inside the bailey, leave a portion of that fog behind to protect your horse. Do you understand?

"Aye," she said, the word nothing more than a breath of sound for she was passing under the portcullis and into the keep.

Walk with that mist surrounding you, Kynni. Let it flow before you as you move and trail behind you so that no one will see your passing. Walk quietly on the balls of your feet, padding as lightly as the wolf stalking its prey. Do not move quickly for you will leave behind a movement of air. Walk calmly, purposefully and turn toward the main gatehouse. The dungeon can only be accessed through the guardroom. There is a stairway there but it is manned. You must send the fog ahead of you and when you do, imagine that fog entering the guards' nostrils, their ears and mouths, every orifice of their bodies. Let it settle within them and lull them into a stupor. When you do, you will be able to pass by them unseen.

Dismounting, Kynthia saw people all around her but no one was looking her way. The fog was not an actual entity but a state of her own mind into which she had enveloped herself and in the doing, removed all traces of her existence from the sight of those around her. She wondered how Cainer Cree had discovered such a marvelous weapon and made a mental note to ask when she could speak with him again.

There were five guards in the main gatehouse. Sitting around a table, playing cards, they were as oblivious to Kynthia's passing as through the bailey. She moved past them like a feather floating upon the wind and was almost to the stairs when she heard the first scream.

"He's got a set of lungs on him, don't he?" one of the guards joked, and the others laughed.

She knew it was Leksi who had screamed and almost let go of her control of the mind-shrouding fog hovering around her. The edges of the fog began to pull back.

He's as good as dead if you lose it, wench! the Reaper shouted in her mind. *Is that what you want?*

Fear for Leksi brought tears to Kynthia's eyes, but she reinforced the strength of the fog. She watched it flow smoothly away from her once more and moved quickly toward the stairs.

"There's a damned draft in here," one of the guards complained. "Shut that door Lykus."

See what I mean? the Reaper cautioned. *Go slowly, wench. You'll get to him in time.*

In time? The words drove straight into her heart and when another scream pierced the walls, she put her hands over her ears.

Steady, wench, Cainer Cree said.

"He is in pain," she whined.

The next scream was cut off in mid-vibrato and Kynthia stopped dead still, her eyes wide. "Cree?" she whispered.

He has passed out. Hurry now, wench. There are no guards between you and where Krull is being kept. Get to him and release him. Now!

"I am not worried about Krull. I want—"

Release Krull, then go after your man. If you wait, Leksi Helios will die and there will be no way to bring him back!

The insistent directions slithering through her mind led Kynthia to the cell where Konan Krull stood with his hands wrapped around the bars, his forehead pressed tightly against the iron. He flinched as she rushed toward him.

"Let go of the bars!" she ordered, following the Reaper's instructions.

Krull was so stunned to see a woman in that terrible place, he could do no more than gawk. When she took hold of the bars and jerked, he laughed. "You've got to be kidding, woman!" he said. Despite the hopelessness he felt having been listening to his captain's screams of agony, the sight of a mere woman trying to open a locked cell by pulling on the bars was hysterically funny to him.

But the Lord High Commander stopped in mid-guffaw when the door not only sprang open but also came completely off its hinges. He blinked as it was tossed away, as though it weighed no more than a feather.

"How the hell did you…?" he began, but was interrupted as the warrioress grabbed his arm and jerked him out of the cell.

"I've no time to answer your stupid questions," she snapped, and began dragging him down the corridor.

If Konan Krull had been astounded at the strength this woman had exhibited when she'd yanked the cell door, he was dumbfounded when she took on two guards single-handedly and sent them into the hereafter without so much as breaking a sweat. He looked down at the dead Nebullians and whistled silently. Broken necks crooked at opposite angles, the warriors lay slumped against the wall to either side of the torture room door as the woman jerked it open and disappeared inside.

The three torturers applying their trade looked up with quizzical expressions on their ugly faces but none rushed to intercept the virago who had blown into the room. They stood where they were — hot pinchers in the hand of one, a cat-o'-nine-tails in the hands of another — and gaped while the third dropped the dagger in his hand and backed away.

"You fucking bastards!" the woman shouted, her eyes wide, lips drawn back over her teeth.

A naked Leksi Helios lay on his belly, strapped to a low iron table, his wrists and ankles circled with wide, heavy bands. His back was a mass of red and black savagely abused flesh with deep cuts from the whip and seared flesh from the pinchers. The upper portion of his thighs had been given the same brutal treatment and the soles of his feet were deeply blistered.

Krull turned his head from the pitiful sight of his captain and looked into the amused eyes of King Abalam Robeus.

"Did you come to take a look at our Pretty Boy, Milord Krull?" the king asked with a smirk. "I can guarantee you he is no longer as tight as he once was."

One of the torturers dared to try to stop the woman from getting to the king. That man met his end when the woman's hand thrust into his chest and the very heart was pulled from his body. At that sight, the second torturer's eyes rolled up in his head and he crumpled to the floor like an overcooked noodle. He did not feel the foot that came down hard on his throat to crush his windpipe.

As the Lord High Commander would later remember, it was the sounds that followed which disturbed him the most. Not the sight of a vengeful woman rushing at the king with hands arched into claws or the sight of her snapping off the head of the remaining torturer who dared stand in her way. Nor was it the sight of that bodiless head being tossed away as though a piece of refuse. It was the sound that would linger in Konan Krull's mind and wake him on dark, bitter nights and propel him to a sitting position, sweat dripping from his handsome brow.

Popping. Creaking. Rasping. Scraping. The sinewy squeal of flesh and cartilage moving—bones breaking and elongating. Jawbones thrusting in a shriek that made the flesh crawl and the hairs stand up on the arms. Fingernails growing at an alarming rate only to become thick, horny plates curved with viciousness and as sharp as a dagger's blade. Bristling fur popping out in squeals of expansion that moved in waves down a body dropped to all fours. Legs shortening, hips and shoulders re-jointing until there was no longer anything even vaguely human about what now stood in the woman's place. With sharp fangs glistening with dripping saliva and red eyes glowing with unspeakable cruelty, the low growl would forever remain in Konan Krull's nightmares to underscore all the sounds that came before.

King Abalam Robeus stared at the transformed woman, his eyes glazed, and his lips trembling. Slowly, he pushed himself from the chair. He took a step to the side and when the beastess did not spring, he braved another. Then another. A faint glimmer lit the king's steady gaze. His chin came up.

"Nice wolfie," the king whispered. "You don't want to hurt Abbie."

Krull switched his attention from the king to the beastess hunched a few feet away. The hackles on the creature's back were standing straight up. Her head was lowered, glaring at the king from under thick, bushy brows. Another low growl came from deep within the wide, furry chest.

"No, you don't want to hurt me," the king repeated. He took another few steps. He jerked his eyes toward a battle-ax hanging upon the torture room wall then looked back at the beastess.

Krull, too, glanced toward the battle-ax but made no move to go after it to keep it out of the king's hands. Instinct had warned him that he would distract the creature from its objective should he move so he stood where he was, drawing in quick, shallow breaths, his hands flexing at his side.

"Nice, nice wolf," the king said. Then he turned to lunge for the battle-ax.

The beastess sprang up on her hind legs and propelled herself forward. Her front legs closed around the king's hips and brought him down—a foot away from the protection of the weapon hanging on the wall.

Backing away from what he thought was about to happen, Krull realized his captain was awake and, with his head turned toward the scene about to unfold before him, smiling weakly.

With infinite care so as not to mar the flesh, the beastess ripped at the clothing of the king and bared his backside. His plump ass lifted into the air as he scrambled to break free. Screaming with fear—his dirt-packed fingernails scraping the stone floor in an attempt to gain purchase—Abalam Robeus was striving to move away from the danger behind him.

But the avenging creature pinning him had no intention of letting him go. With one savage swipe of its mouth, she tore off both the king's nether cheeks. The agonized shriek that followed reverberated through the torture room and a sickening stench wafted through the air as the lower intestine pulled free of the man's body along with his flesh.

"Gave new meaning to ripping him a new one," Krull would later joke.

Aye, Krull thought as he watched the unbelievable spectacle playing itself out—it was the sounds that would forever remain in his consciousness.

The yowls of agony ripping from the throat of Abalam Robeus, the snarls of the beastess as it devoured the thrashing man.

The smacking. The crunching. The wet sloshing noises that turned the stomach. The resonance of veins snapping and heart snatched from a splintered rib cage.

When the last agonized scream had faded and what was left of the king lay oozing upon the floor, it was the loud, piercing howl of conquest that broke from the creature's throat that would become the stuff of nightmares for the Lord High Commander of the Venturian Forces.

And it would be many years before he could free himself of the sight of woman turning to beast then turning back again in the blink of an eye. As he stared at her, Kynthia transformed. Hunkered down before him—naked as the day she had been born and covered in the blood and gore of her vanquished enemy—she turned her head and looked up at Krull.

As brave as any man to walk the face of the earth, Konan Krull knew the only moment of sheer terror he had ever experienced as he stared into the brutal eyes of Leksi's woman.

"Is…he…alive?" she managed to say, for the fangs had not yet retracted into her mouth.

Krull shifted his gaze from her to Leksi. "I think so," he whispered.

Wearily, she got to her feet and padded over to her lover. She knew before she ever laid hands to him that he was dying. His eyes were open but were fixed, the pupils dilated.

"Come here, warrior," she told Krull.

The Lord High Commander swallowed hard before taking a few steps toward her. When she glanced back at him with impatience, he felt his bowels threaten to loosen.

"Come here!" she ordered.

He would later tell his beloved Isabell that it wasn't fear that propelled him forward as though shot from a cannon. It was the look in the woman's eye.

"Take up that dagger," she said, "and make a cut here." She put her hand on Leksi's back. "Not too deep. About half an inch."

"What?" Krull questioned, his forehead creased.

"Just do it, fool!" she thundered.

Stooping to pick up the dagger one of the torturers had been using on Leksi, he took a quick look at the warrior and knew he was beyond help. Nevertheless, he did as he was ordered though cutting Helios hurt Krull's heart.

Astounding Krull further, the woman stretched out on the floor on her belly. "Now cut me in the same place, but deeper."

His mouth open, eyebrows raised, Krull was about to protest but again the look she shot him stopped him. He squatted down beside her and used the blade on her smooth back, wincing as she flinched from the pain.

"Spread the flesh apart until you can get your fingers inside the cut."

Krull would later tell Kratos that he thought the woman had lost her mind. He would have balked at her demand if she had not been glaring up at him with eyes that dared him to disobey so he did as he was told. He told Kratos—

"I had to make the incision wider to get my hand inside. I knew I was hurting her but it was what she wanted, what she demanded I do. She instructed me on how to pull the flesh apart and what to look for inside her. When I found that grayish-green honeycomb of wriggling bodies nested inside her, I had to turn away and throw up."

"Pull one out and be quick about it, Krull. He's dying!"

The writhing thing he drew up from the woman's body was the most disgusting, hideous thing he had ever seen. It lashed against his hand—its spiked tail slashing at his flesh—and the triangular head whipped back and forth. The slit of a mouth with its fierce rows of tiny teeth tried to bite him.

"Drop it on the warrior's back," she ordered. "Now!"

Krull did not give himself time to question that order. He wanted to get rid of the thing in his hand so he took a quick step to the table upon which Leksi lay bound and practically threw the loathsome creature onto the dying warrior's back.

Staring with shocked eyes as wide as saucers, Krull watched the beast lift the upper portion of its body then dive into the warrior's back, disappearing quickly.

"Is it in?" she asked weakly.

"Aye," Krull replied, the gorge rising in his throat.

"Then leave us," she said. "You should not be here when he Transitions for the first time."

"Transitions?" he questioned.

Forcing his eyes from Leksi to the woman pushing herself up from the floor, Krull could not believe what he was seeing. The wide, deep cut he had made into the woman's back had closed up as though it had never been made. Despite the caked blood around where the wound had been made, her flesh was as unblemished as the rest of her.

"Can't you do anything you're told without being browbeaten into it?" she snarled at him as she gained her feet. She reached out to shove him. "Get the hell out of here!"

Krull narrowed his eyes. "You're a bossy little bitch, aren't you?" he asked.

"Go," she said, waving him away. "I can control him—you can't."

One look at Leksi Helios told Krull no one would ever control the warrior again. His eyes were open, staring, glazing in death. His chest had ceased to move.

"Wench," he began but she turned her back on him.

Grief was welling up inside Konan Krull for he loved Leksi like a brother. To have had the warrior die in such a horrible way brought out the berserker in the Lord High Commander.

"I want to kill every last one of them," he said, tears flooding his eyes.

"Then go do it if you think you can, else stay outside and wait for us. Not even the warrior and I together can slay the lot of the Pleiadesians. It will take the Sisters and your people to help us."

Krull shrugged away what he thought was a stupid remark. It was true the Venturians would need the help of the Amazeens and Hell Hags as well as the Daughters of the Multitude to crush Abalam's war troops. In order for that to happen, he and the woman needed to quit Nebul and go back to bring their own forces to bear against the murdering horde.

"I'll wait outside," he said listlessly.

Kynthia laid the backs of her fingers on Leksi's still cheek. "Reaper?" she whispered.

Give the fledgling time to heal him, wench. Your man will survive.

Cainer Cree's voice was soft and encouraging in her ear. She believed him for he had no reason to lie to her. Bending down, she placed a gentle kiss on Leksi's brow then set about unshackling his wrists and ankles. When his limbs were free, she knelt down beside him and waited for the Transition she knew would come.

* * * * *

Krull was squatting down with his back to the wall. His forehead was braced on his arms. He had repeated the Litany of the Wind for Leksi twice and had started on the third recitation for the Repose of the Warrior's Soul when he heard the sounds begin once more in the torture room down the corridor from him.

Tiredly, he lifted his head and listened, his face turned toward those sickening sounds. A part of him wondered if she was devouring Leksi's body and he knew anger almost as fierce as the one that had caused his grief. Another part of him thought perhaps that was the best way to send Leksi to the Realm of the Wind. Let him forever be a part of the woman he loved so deeply. In a way, the warrior would live on.

At least as long as the she-creature drew breath.

After a while, when the howl of victory came, Krull closed his eyes and lowered his head to his arms once more. He was bone-tired, sick of spirit and his heart ached with a sorrow he knew would never leave him for as long as he lived.

"Never is a long time, my friend."

Very slowly, the Lord High Commander raised his head, and when he looked up, his eyes grew wide and his face lost its natural ruddy color. His lips parted.

"Let's get out of here, warrior," Kynthia demanded. "We should be able to get past the guards easily with the both of us casting fog."

"Is that like farting, wench?" asked a laughing voice.

Krull could only stare at Leksi Helios. He knew the warrior had died. There was no doubt in his mind.

"Do you see even one little bruise on his body, warrior?" Kynthia asked with an amused snort.

Staring at the man standing before him, Krull could find not one mark upon his naked body. There were no cuts or scrapes, no burns or bruises. There wasn't even any blood streaking his flesh.

"I laved him with my tongue as any she-wolf would her mate," the woman remarked as though she had read his mind. "That's why he's so clean."

Krull's face screwed up with distaste at the remark and he swallowed hard. He gagged, and pushed up to his feet and turned his face away.

"He's going to heave, wench," Leksi warned and pushed his lady back.

They watched the Lord High Commander relieve his gut of whatever was left in it then gently took his arms in their hands.

"I've of a mind to get out of here, Your Grace," Kynthia said as they ushered Krull down the hall, one to either side of him. "How 'bout you?"

"I'd like to find at least a pair of britches first, wench," Leksi said, his face burning.

"I like you well enough naked, milord," Kynthia responded with a giggle.

"Aye, well, my dangly is cold," Leksi complained.

"Oh, my!" came a gasp.

The trio looked back to see Princess Clea standing like a statue, a hand to her mouth. Her eyes were wide as she stared at Leksi's unclothed body.

"Wench, do something!" Leksi whined.

Shrugging—her face stretched with a wide grin—Kynthia lifted her arm and mist rose up from the floor, obscuring them from Clea's shocked stare.

"She'll think she dreamed it," Kynthia said as they walked quickly past the woman.

Leksi looked back over his shoulder at Clea as the Princess fanned the thick mist in a concerted effort to clear away the obstruction.

"She's trying to get another look at your dangly, warrior," Kynthia laughed.

"I need britches!" Leksi stated, his eyes flashing amber fire. "My cock is cold!"

"Take matters into your own hands, then, and shut the hell up," Konan hissed.

It took the trio but a few extra moments to find a guard room and allow Leksi and Kynthia time to find clothing and dress. All the while, Clea was stumbling down the corridor, her arms windmilling in front of her as she tried to find her way through the thick mist.

* * * * *

Cainer Cree stretched out on the cliff overlooking Achasán Island. He was lying on his belly, staring at *The Levant*, the airship that had brought him to this accursed land, his chin propped in the cup of his hands. His youngest Reaper was safe with her mate and riding alongside the one called Krull on their way to the Amazeen lands.

The Reaper sighed. His work with Kynthia was over. Like any good parent, Cree knew he needed to cut the apron strings so he made a vow not to answer Kynthia should she seek him out again unless it was vitally important. It would be up to her to teach Leksi Helios what he needed to know about being a Reaper.

As he had with almost all the other seekers whom he had made into creatures like him, he felt sadness at the severing of the parental bonds. He would miss the interaction and would once more know the bitter loneliness of his position until the next seeker came to ask his help.

"You would not know such loneliness if you had not denied me, my sweet deargs dul."

The voice was sultry with a deep tone that made his staff move.

"Have you brought me another seeker?" he asked, not looking up at the goddess who had stepped down from the vastness of the heavens to torment him.

Morrigunia, Goddess of Life, Death and War came to sit beside her prisoner. She wore a voluminous gown shot through with delicate silver threads. In her long blonde hair, she wore a circlet of pale pink flowers knotted amongst ivy.

"There is one waiting but it will be a while before I send him your way," his wardeness replied. "He's not ready yet." She cocked her head to one side. "What think you of the female Reaper you made?"

"No more women," he vowed. "Not from my body, anyway."

"Not directly from your body, perhaps," she said. "But there is another, made just this week, I believe."

"Khnum's doing," the Reaper said with distaste. "Her name is Neith."

"Ah, yes. Neith. She is one to be watched."

"Khnum needs killing," he told her.

"He was the first one you made, wasn't he?" she asked.

"Aye," he replied, his teeth grinding. "You brought him to me before I even knew what all this was about and he has made an entire race of Reapers."

"The Ordonese," she sighed. "That was a mistake on my part to allow that to happen, but all will be set to rights eventually. That tribe will die out."

There was a long silence between them then Morrigunia turned to look out at the flying ship.

"Are you still writing in your journal, my beloved?"

The Reaper cast her a hateful look. "How could I when you took it from me long ago, Morrigunia?" He narrowed his eyes. "What did you do with it, anyway?"

She shrugged. "It is safe for now. When it is needed, it will surface."

"Khnum has it, doesn't he?" the Reaper snarled.

She put her index finger to her chin. "No one has it, beloved. It is safe upon its shelf until it will be needed."

"Another mistake on your part. It outlines how the Transferences are to be made. It is a dangerous piece of work."

"*You* are a dangerous piece of work, my deargs dul," she giggled.

He ignored her comment. Getting up, he dusted his hands together, his gaze locked on the ship he so longed to be able to fly. Turning his back, he walked away from that punishing sight and the tormentress who made his life a living hell.

Chapter Twelve

Flavia died with a smirk on her ugly face and the secret of why she had wanted the plan to oust Abalam Robeus from power to fail buried deep in her evil mind. Despite two hours of prolonged torture—water dripping upon her head the only torture allowed under Amazeen Tribunal Law—she went to her grave without revelations of any kind.

Stymied and angry that she had not garnered the information she sought, Deianeira, the defense queen, stared out across the night-darkened battlements of Androdameia, the keep that was the capitol of Amazeen, and ground her teeth.

"There was a reason she did this," her sister, Queen Antianeira observed.

"Aye, well, we'll never know what it is now!" Deianeira grumbled.

"Who was to know she had heart problems?"

Deianeira turned a glare to her sister. "Did she die of a heart ailment or was she helped along?"

"What are you saying? Do you think someone murdered her?"

"Who was the last person to see her in the dungeon?" the defense queen countered.

Antianeira thought about it for a moment. "Was it Harmothoe?"

"Aye, our virtuous Abbess of the Womanly Arts," her sister replied. "She went there to reason with Flavia. Instead, I believe she went there to make sure she did not answer our questions."

"But why?"

Deianeira shook her head. "I have no idea but perhaps we need to question Harmothoe."

"They have never been close that I could see," Antianeira commented. "I hardly ever saw them speaking to one another."

"What better way for conspirators to behave toward one another?"

The domestic queen chewed on her lower lip. "As I recall Harmothoe voted no to the plan to help the Venturians."

"Think back, Sister," Deianeira said. "Wasn't there a time when Harmothoe journeyed to Tasjorn quite often? She would go disguised as an itinerant nun or some such. Do you remember that?"

Antianeira nodded slowly. "Aye, I do recall something of that."

"And tell me this—how did Flavia know Queen Mona had slept with Lord Krull? Would that not be quite the secret in Ventura? It would have had to have happened after Krull married Isabell, don't you agree?"

"To my knowledge, Flavia never left the borders of Amazeen," Antianeira said. "How *would* she have known unless someone told her?"

"How, indeed?"

Turning to look out over the moon-silvered waters of the Molpadia River that wound its serpentine way south, the domestic queen's forehead was wrinkled with concern. "I would not have imagined a man such as Lord Krull to betray his marriage vows. From all I have heard, he is an honorable man."

Her sister snorted. "Even honorable men get horny, Sister."

"Aye, but Mona is not a woman I think of being capable to stir such lust in a man like that."

"Who knows? Perhaps she drugged him. I wouldn't put anything past those Hell Hags."

"Mona would not do that." At her sister's look of disbelief, Antianeira raised her chin. "I know her better than you, and I tell you she would not stoop to drug a man in order to sleep with him."

"Even to get a child from him?" Deianeira suggested. "That was a common practice with the Daughters of the Night in Mona's mother's time just as it is common practice with us today."

"If you remember, Mona outlawed such things when she took the throne. I can not see her breaking her own rule."

Deianeira sighed. "Aye, well Krull is one helluva handsome man. Any woman would find lust for him oozing through her loins. If she didn't drug him, perhaps she enticed him in another way. It's possible, you know."

"Still," Antianeira said, "I find it strange he would cast aside the woman he supposedly loves more than life for a tumble with a woman who means nothing to him." She looked at her twin. "Don't you?"

"Men have done stranger things when they think with their cocks," the defense queen replied. "She could have caught him at a low point in his marriage. That happens and men stray."

The sisters were quiet as clouds slid across the moon and a freshening breeze blew their long, unbound hair about their faces.

"One thing I have always wondered about," Deianeira said as she leaned her elbows on a merlon of the crenellated wall. "Who was Lilit's father?"

Antianeira drew in a long breath. "It wasn't Konan Krull, if that is where this is going."

"I've heard it was a demon. Do you know who it was?"

"I never knew his name. He was no demon but a vampyre and the very worst of his kind according to Mona."

Deianeira looked at her sister. "A vampyre?"

"So I was told. He took Mona savagely, nearly tearing her apart in the process. It was a wonder he did not turn her into one of his own kind for that is what I hear those bastards do."

"So that is Lilit's heritage?" Deianeira said. "When she is of age, will she then become like her sire?"

"Most likely and will begin turning the Daughters like herself, no doubt. She seems to enjoy taking blood I hear."

"I suppose that is the main reason I don't care for the Hell Hags to begin with. They use blood drinking in their rituals." Deianeira shuddered. "That makes me ill just thinking of it."

"Aye, well, taking a sip here and there is a hell of a lot different than draining it from a victim's neck. They are no threat to us," Antianeira remarked.

"Not like the potential problem we have that Flavia perpetrated," the defense queen reminded her sister.

"We can discuss this all night, but the fact remains that Flavia is dead and we are no closer to learning the motivation for her treason. Perhaps you should bring Harmothoe before the Tribunal and ask if she had something to do with Flavia's death."

"I never liked Harmothoe," Deianeira said. "I well remember her making me redo that damned doily five times before she was satisfied I had crocheted it to her specifications!" Her face turned hard. "I ripped out those stitches four times! Who the hell needs a doily anyway? And why does a warrioress need to know how to crochet?"

Antianeira smiled. "To smooth her rough edges, perhaps?"

"It will give me pleasure to question that bitch." Deianeira grinned nastily. "At least five times!"

* * * * *

Lilit waved away the messenger who had come to bring news of the death of Flavia Pantasriste, the Amazeen Abbess of Education. Despite her lack of regard for anyone other than herself, the young princess knew a moment—brief though it was—of unhappiness at the news. She threw the missive into the fire then slumped in her chair, her long, skinny legs thrust out in front of her. Pouting, she drummed her fingers on the chair arm.

"What will you do now, Highness?" the shadow clinging to the wall asked.

"It is my sire's wish that Konan Krull meet his end in the dungeon of Nebul. I promised him I would see to it!" Lilit snapped.

The shadow slid down the wall, its talons plucking at the stone. When it slithered to the floor, it stood upright, its wings folded primly at its sides. "Do you have an assignment for me, then, Your Majesty?"

Lilit swung her black gaze to the bat-woman who hovered nearby. "I can not travel to Amazeen on my own and my worthless mother will not make the trek again until it is time to make war on the Pleiadesians."

"Youth has its disadvantages," the shadow said with a sigh.

"Aye, I won't be there to allow that old witch to have her sick way with me again. If I were there, she would meet her end very quickly whilst in the throes of her disgusting passion. Thus, I think you should silence Harmothoe before she spills my father's preparations to the Amazeen."

The bat-woman crept closer. "Would you like me to soothe you before I go, Your Majesty?" She licked her thin lips. "It would calm you and you would sleep better, I think."

"No, Amenirdis, I would not!" Lilit spat. She lashed out with her foot and kicked the bat-woman in the chest, sending her crashing backward.

Amenirdis got to her knees and with long fingers twined as though in prayer, begged her young mistress' forgiveness. She cringed as Lilit got to her feet, her dark eyes flashing fire.

"I let Harmothoe have her repulsive way with me so I could set my father's plan into motion. Never again will I let a female touch my flesh! Now find that old crone and make sure she does not reveal our plans to her Sisters!"

The bat-woman bowed her head in acknowledgement of the order and slipped silently to the window. Opening the portal, she hopped up on the sill then launched herself into the heavens, her wings flapping.

"Vile creature," Lilit said with a shudder. The twelve year old marched to the window and shut it, latching it securely against the return of the bat-woman. "How do you stand such beasts, Father?"

One must use the arsenal at one's command, Daughter, an oily voice whispered in the young girl's ear.

"When I am queen, I—"

Before you can rule, you must learn to obey, Daughter, the voice snapped. *What I ordered you to accomplish was not done!*

Lilit flinched. "Krull was not captured by the Nebullian Troopers? I thought—"

A blood-drinker rescued Krull and his captain! The words thundered so loudly in the girl's ears, she slapped her hands against them and fell to her knees. *A mere woman dared to foil my plans!*

"Who is she, Father? Give me her name, tell me where to find her, and I will send my lieutenants Amenirdis and Hekat after her."

A vicious laugh echoed through Lilit's head and brought a tiny trickle of blood oozing from both ears.

Too late! the voice screamed. *It was a vile female Reaper who dared this!*

Lilit could feel her father's fury like a cold, wet mantle thrown over her shoulders. She sagged against the weight of it and lay down, curling into a fetal position with her thumb stuck between her lips. The stench of his breath washed over and she shuddered and began trembling violently.

You will learn, you worthless female! the voice bellowed at her. *I should not have entrusted anything to you until you are ripe with the blood!*

Lying upon the cold floor, the young girl began to hum to herself. Her mind was filled with all manner of vile images of torture, death and destruction. She could smell the brimstone bubbling all around her and feel it seeping into her pores. She whimpered, knowing she had failed her powerful sire this time.

For her sire's people, the Ordonese, there would be no easy conquest of Pleiades now. With Krull alive and at the head of the joint forces, the Venturians would assemble to place Clea — a stupid woman — upon the Pleiadesian throne. There would be no man for Lilit to seduce when she became ripe with the blood.

"Clea," Lilit whispered with loathing. "May your cunt rot, you barren cow!"

Her thoughts turned from the ugly Clea to Krull and memory of the night she had hidden in her mother's room at the inn in Tasjorn reared up to prod her with evil fingers.

That night she remembered, her lips curling with distaste, her mother had risen at a scratch upon her door. She had opened wide the door and allowed Konan Krull inside.

"I don't have long, Mona," Krull had said. "What did you need to speak with me about?"

"You look hot, Lord Krull. Perhaps a cool glass of milk to refresh you?"

Despite the warrior's protest, her mother had hurried to the table. Taking a flagon from a bowl of ice, she poured milk into a golden goblet. She held it out to Krull and insisted he ease his thirst.

"Stupid man," Lilit sneered. "You never suspected a thing!"

The goblet had held a stiff measure of tenerse and that drug mixed with the milk had brought about nearly instant lust in the warrior, and he had fallen upon the queen and dragged her to the floor.

"Whoring bitch," the young girl accused.

Her mother had drugged the Lord High Commander. She had lain with him and spread her legs, allowing that heathen stud to thrust his slippery cock between her whoring thighs. She had clawed his back, spurring him on, and cooed vulgar suggestions in his ear. His panting and grunts matched his seducer's groans and sighs. The slap of their lower bodies against one another was forceful and loud in the room. She had reveled in his loathsome touch and had cried out in pleasure when his weapon had spurted inside her.

"Harlot!" Lilit hissed. "Filthy hag! How dare you cuckold my father!"

Pounding her fists upon the stone beneath her, the young girl called her mother every vile name she could think of. Hatred spewed from her lips like the gush of pus from an infected wound.

It did not matter to Lilit that Lord Krull had been forced into taking her mother. That he had had no control over his lust because of the drug made no difference to the young girl. He was a guilty as her mother, though to this day Lilit could remember the mortal shame of what he had done stamped on his handsome features.

"What did you do?" she remembered him demanding in a shocked voice.

"I wanted a boy child," Lilit's mother replied. "I wanted *your* boy child!"

"You bitch!" Krull accused. "I helped you and this is what you do to repay me?"

"I need a boy child to help me rule," her mother insisted. "My women are not warrioresses like the Amazeen and we have been invaded many times. I need a strong hand at my right side." She held out her hands. "Our son will be as great a defender for us as you are for Ventura."

"Get away from me!" Krull shouted as he threw open the door and stumbled from the room, his face stricken, eyes haunted.

The queen, indeed, had conceived a child from that wanton night but Lilit had made sure the get did not survive. Calling upon her father for help, she had been sent a brew that would cause her mother to abort the thing growing inside her. Not only did the brew destroy the boy child, it withered her mother's womb and made it barren.

There would be no more brats slithering from between her unfaithful mother's thighs. There would be no boy child with whom to scrapple over the power of Queen Mona's monarchy.

"Not that a male could ever rule the Daughters of the Night!" Lilit mumbled.

Consigning Konan Krull to the deepest pit of the Abyss, the child fell into a troubled doze, dreaming of the day she would one day rule the Daughters. With her sire's help, she would extend that rule over all the earth.

Chapter Thirteen

No doubt Clea would alert her father's men once she made her way into the dungeon and found his mutilated body. As smart a woman as she was, she would have the Tribunal swear her in as ruler of Pleiades before word got out that the king was dead.

"There will be hell to pay in Nebul this night," Konan remarked. "They won't know who—or what—entered the keep and murdered the king and his henchmen."

"Clea will know," Kynthia said. "She'll realize she wasn't dreaming when she saw Leksi in the buff."

"Let's hope no innocent gets snagged in their net," Leksi commented, ignoring his lady's dig.

"They'll be too busy protecting their new queen, I'd wager, to do much of anything before we return."

"What will happen when our forces invade Pleiades?" Kynthia asked. "Will Clea surrender without a fight?"

"She will no doubt see the advantage of it," Konan replied. "At least I hope she will."

"Do you not think we should send an emissary, Your Grace?" Leksi inquired. "Let her know we have no intention of usurping her power amongst her people."

"Aye but that we will not countenance things being the way they were under her insane father," Kynthia suggested.

"Who should I send?" Konan asked.

"Let me go," Leksi volunteered. At Kynthia's protest, he turned to her. "Do I not have powers such as you have, wench?"

Kynthia frowned. "Aye, and most likely your powers are superior to mine since you are a male."

"Then why worry about my safety?"

"Who said I was?" she countered.

"Can I not read your mind as easily as you once read mine?"

The warrioress shrugged. "I'll have to be more careful with my thoughts, warrior."

Konan was listening closely to the lovers' exchange. He still could not look that closely at his captain without wonder. There was not a single blemish on Leksi Helios' flesh and—if truth be told—he looked younger than he had before they had ridden out from Ventura.

"When reapers age, they do so very slowly. How old would you say I am?" Kynthia asked.

A strained look appeared on Konan's face. "Lass, I learned long ago to never speculate on a lady's age, but I'd say no more than twenty, twenty-five at the most."

"I am thirty-two, milord," Kynthia informed the Lord High Commander. "Leksi will not age past the way he looks right now for at least another hundred. Neither will I."

Konan shook his head. "This is new to me, wench. I have yet to get my mind around it all."

They had reined in their mounts and were sitting upon a rise that overlooked the Pleiadesian keep at Nebul. Even from that distance, they could see people scurrying about and as they watched, Abalam Robeus' standard was drawn down from the battlements to be replaced by the personal insignia of his daughter.

"She'll be a fine ruler," Konan commented.

"What do you wish for me to tell her, Your Grace?"

"I didn't say I was sending you," Konan said with a frown. "Do you remember where you were just an hour ago?"

Leksi shrugged. "Aye, but that was an hour ago and before I had gained the strength of ten men."

"And the arrogance of them as well," Kynthia mumbled.

"What do you think, wench?" Konan asked, turning to her. "Do you think we can trust them not to lop off his head?"

"I'll go with him," Kynthia declared. "That way I know he'll be safe."

"What of me, then?" the Lord High Commander asked.

"Queen Mona and the Amazeen queens have warrioresses on their way at this very moment. Stay here and intercept them but make sure they are ranged along this rise so Queen Clea will see we mean business."

"Good thinking, wench," Leksi said. "A show of force can only seal the deal."

"I'd like to see the faces of those who captured us when they see you riding back in," Konan said.

"They won't see him returning any more than they saw us leaving," Kynthia reminded Krull. "Until we are in Queen Clea's presence, I don't think it wise to let her warriors know we are there."

"Another good point," Konan agreed. "Perhaps I should commission you with the Venturian Forces, milady."

"Kratos would like that," Leksi chuckled.

"It's a good thing that handsome soldier wasn't with you when the two of you were captured," Kynthia said. "They would have killed him."

"Handsome?" Konan repeated, his brows lifted.

"She thinks so," Leksi replied.

"Aye, well, he is," Kynthia stated. She jerked on the reins and turned her mount toward the path down from the rise. "You coming, warrior?"

Konan and Leksi smiled in unison as they watched the young woman's rear shifting from side-to-side as the horse made its way down the path.

"You've got your hands full there, Helios," Konan said.

"Aye, Your Grace, and what a handful that arse is going to be!" Leksi concurred then put his heels to his stallion's flanks.

Konan crossed his hands over the pommel and leaned forward, watching the two as they made their way down to the road that led to Nebul. Behind him, he heard the pounding of hooves and when he turned his head, he saw the personal standard of Queen Mona of the Daughters of the Night. A thick ribbon of dust trailed off to her right.

"The Amazeens are here," the Lord High Commander said to his steed then reached down to pat the horse's neck.

By the time Queen Deianeira drew into position on his left, Queen Mona was reining in beside him to the right. He greeted the warrioresses with respect.

"You mount a truly substantial force, miladies," he complimented them, for there were hundreds of women ranged in a fan-shape behind the two busty queens.

"Lady Kynthia's aunt will be here shortly with her troop," Queen Mona said. "Her horse threw a shoe and she had to procure a new mount."

"Lady Kynthia and Lord Leksi have gone back down there," Konan commented.

"Back down there?" Queen Deianeira questioned. She narrowed her eyes. "You look none the worse for wear so I presume you escaped without a trip to Robeus' chamber of horrors."

"Not so, I'm afraid," the Lord High Commander said. "They tortured Leksi for well over an hour. Lady Kynthia arrived just in the nick of time for he had…" He stopped and coughed, unsure whether he should say anything about Leksi having died.

"She made him One with the Blood?" Queen Mona asked.

"I suppose so," he answered.

"Well, it had to be if they are to be Joined," the Amazeen defense queen stated. "It wouldn't have worked out otherwise."

"I will be eternally grateful for the lady's intervention," Konan said. "I don't think Robeus had any intention of either Leksi or I ever leaving his infernal keep."

"No, he did not," Queen Deianeira stated. "He wanted you out of the way so he could turn Ventura over to the vampyres."

Konan blinked. "What are you saying?"

"My daughter's sire," Queen Mona said, her face crinkled with what could only be disgust, "has a great desire to rule the entire world. I did not know that until one of his minions confessed it to Deianeira."

"Under a great deal of persuasion, she told me," the Amazeen defense queen said. She smiled nastily. "She died while being persuaded, I fear."

"The vampyres reside in Ordon, do they not?" Konan asked. "High up in the Transeld Mountains?"

"Slowly but surely they are making their way down to the valley where the common folk live. Sekhem has every intention of being Lord and Master of all he surveys. For years he has tried to find a Reaper from whom he could harvest a fledgling but as yet, he has not."

"Aren't they one and the same?" Konan asked, his brow furrowed.

"I can only tell you what I have heard. Some of it may be fact and some legend. Some of it may simply be wishful thinking on the part of the storyteller but from what I have learned Reapers drink blood to survive. They do not attack humans for the hell of it as vampyres do," Queen Deianeira said. "Nor do they kill indiscriminately whatever living thing crosses their path."

"I have heard vampyres cannot be killed. Is that true?"

"Contrary to folklore, vampyres are not all that powerful," Mona replied. "They can not venture into daylight, a Reaper can. Thus, they are limited to the night. They spend their days locked in coffins and at the mercy of anyone who might happen upon them. They are vulnerable at that time and can be slain easily with a stake to the heart."

"Reapers can die but only when their parasite has been damaged beyond its ability to repair itself," the defense queen added.

"Vampyres have more fear of humans than Reapers do."

"Unless the entire world is like them," Konan surmised. "Then they would have no one to fear."

"Aye and that is what Sekhem wants. But first, he would like to find a Reaper and he will not stop until he does, mark my words," Mona told him.

* * * * *

Leksi was listening to the conversation taking place upon the rise and was unsettled by the implications. He glanced at Kynthia and saw that she, too, had heard what was being discussed.

"Is this something we need to be concerned about, wench?"

Kynthia shook her head. "I don't know but I will ask Cree when next I—"

I wasn't going to commune with you any longer, Kynthia, but this is something you need to know. The man has been found and he is already one of us, wench.

Kynthia flinched as the bold words slithered into her mind. "You are sure?"

As sure as I am confined on this damnable island, wench.

"Do you know by whom?"

Lord Khnum is the treasonous bastard's name and he will implant fledglings in many of Sekhem's cronies before the year is out, Cainer Cree replied. *What is worse, Khnum has my journal which he was helped to steal when he came here.*

"Why is that of importance?" Leksi asked, trying out his newfound ability to send mental messages.

Because it has the knowledge of Transitioning within its pages, Helios! came the fierce reply.

"And Khnum will use that knowledge to make many more Reapers," Kynthia said with a groan.

Nay, not Reapers such as you and I, but vampyre lords, Cree stated. *A hybrid worse than anything nature could create.*

"Vampyres who can walk in the light of day," Kynthia whispered.

Aye, Cree agreed. *The very worst kind of inhuman monster!*

"We will take care of that later," Leksi reminded them. "Let's get this over with before we—"

There is nothing you can do, anyway, Helios, Cree interrupted. *It will be settled but not for many years. It is not Sekhem we have to worry about but his seed. Concentrate on the matter at hand.*

Kynthia and Leksi could feel Cree pulling back from their minds and looked at one another. "He is worried," Kynthia said.

"With good reason, I think," Leksi agreed. "Who did he mean? Who is Sekhem's seed?"

"I think he means Mona's daughter, Lilit. I have heard it said she will inherit her father's powers when she reaches puberty. She'll one day rule the Hell Hags and that might be a terrible fate for the Daughters. Perhaps she is the one we should go after when this is done."

"You may be right, wench," Leksi agreed.

Leksi rode beside his lady, testing his mental powers and growing easier with them with each passing moment. Though the thought of having to daily drink blood made him a bit ill, he came to terms with it. Just knowing he would have abilities that would make him a superior warrior eased his mind. Contemplating his new strengths, his grin grew wider.

"You run the risk of becoming arrogant, warrior," Kynthia warned him as she intercepted his thoughts.

"Not arrogant but confident, wench," Leksi corrected. "Think of the good such powers can do."

"I think, also, of the harm they can do," his lady warned. "There have been many times I have had to rein in my anger to keep it from lashing out when it shouldn't."

"Then help me control my powers, wench," Leksi said. "Keep me grounded."

Kynthia's heart swelled with love for such a request was a true indication of how much Leksi trusted and respected her.

"And stop thinking on what happened to me," he told her. "You could not have prevented it."

Pain drove through Kynthia's soul. "Just knowing you were in pain…"

"Pain I handled well enough," Leksi said, squirming in the saddle. "Though I am mortified that I screamed like a little girl."

"Do you want to talk about it?" she asked, sensing he did. "Releasing a scream or two did not make you less a man, warrior."

"Perhaps not," Leksi said, "but it will haunt me."

"Why?"

He shrugged. "I thought myself above such things," he admitted. "I always thought if the time came, I would be able to keep my mouth shut and endure it." He winced. "Obviously I wasn't the man I thought I was."

Kynthia reined in her mount and turned to look at him. "Don't say such things, warrior. No human could have withstood the agony that had been inflicted upon you. I doubt even a Reaper could have endured it without screaming. There is no shame in that."

"Venturian warriors are trained early on to resist for as long as they can. I don't think I resisted long enough to be satisfied I didn't give up too soon."

"Your body was a mass of cuts and burns!" Kynthia exclaimed. "How soon would soon be in your mind, Helios?"

Once more Leksi shrugged. "It will take me a while to come to terms with it, wench. I doubt it will happen again, but should it, will the deargs dul within me make it easier for me to bear the pain?"

Kynthia shook her head. "I can't answer that, but why dwell on it, Leksi?"

"I am a warrior, wench. My pride was in my ability to stand firm when confronted with torture. I was trained to do so. I swore an oath that I would hold firm. I didn't meet that challenge well."

"You died!" Kynthia shouted at him, her eyes blazing. "How well do you think you meet death, warrior?"

Sensing the fury building in his lady and the guilt that she had been unable to prevent his agony, he reached out with his newfound power to soothe her mind but she mentally pulled away from him, refusing to allow him to comfort her in that fashion.

"Don't do that," she hissed at him. "Let me wallow in my guilt as you are wallowing in yours."

Leksi flinched. "Is that what I'm doing?"

"Get over it," Kynthia spat. "What is done is done. I could not have prevented it so I have to resign myself to that. You could not have stopped from screaming as agony was being inflicted upon you, and you have to accept that, as well!" She glared at him for a long moment, neither speaking.

Finally, the warrior nodded. "Aye, you are right."

"Of course, I am," she said, kicking her mount into a trot. "I always will be!"

Leksi rolled his eyes as he drummed his heels against his horse's flanks. "Wench, we need to work on *your* arrogance!"

* * * * *

As Cainer Cree paced the sand, the waves of the Chalean Sea lapped eagerly toward his boots. The parasite inside his body was agitated at him being so close to the running water and was causing the Reaper pain in the small of his back.

"Punish me, you bitch," Cree ground out. "I should suffer even greater agony for having given Khnum one of your beastlets!"

The Queen twisted viciously along his spine and Cree went to his knees, a hand to his back as he knelt there and panted with the torment rippling through him.

"Why do you persist in antagonizing the demoness, Beloved?"

Cainer refused to look around at the speaker whose sultry voice slithered through his head like a deadly viper. "Leave me alone, Morrigunia. Haven't you caused enough mischief?"

The Chalean Goddess of Life, Death and War waded out into the waves and bent down to run her hands through the salty foam. "I know what I am about, my deargs dul. Why do you question me?"

He looked up to find Morrigunia's gauzy gown plastered to her luscious curves. There might as well have been nothing covering her for the very outline of her body was in plain view behind the wet material. Despite his ironclad will, his body responded to the sight of the dark red-gold patch of hair at her groin and he turned away, digging his nails into the palms of his hands.

"Such unneeded torment you put yourself through, Cain," she sighed. "All you need do is—"

"Leave!" he shouted. "I hate the sight of you!"

"Well, your cock doesn't," the goddess snapped, but before he could yell at her again, she disappeared in a whirlwind of tiny sparkling lights that drifted out to sea like butterflies.

Tears welled up in Cainer Cree's eyes and he threw back his head and howled to the heavens. His terrible loneliness felt like a boulder pressing down upon his heart and he could barely draw breath. He hurt in his very soul and the honorable warrior inside him was awash in guilt. He had unwittingly made a horrible mistake in allowing Khnum to harvest a fledgling from his, Cainer's, body. In a moment of pique, Morrigunia had allowed him to see into the future and to witness the exacting repercussions his mistake had brought to the world. So overcome with his guilt, he looked once more to the sea and took a step toward its heaving waves.

Instantaneous pain flooded the Reaper's body but he ignored it and kept walking. Had not the Goddess appeared in front of him, he would have flung himself into the pounding waves.

"No," Morrigunia said, lashing out with a palm to Cree's cheek. "This I will not allow!"

Even though the parasite was torturing him, sending bright flashes of intense agony through his spine, Cainer Cree tried to go around the Goddess. The intention of drowning himself was clear in his amber eyes.

"I said no!" she said, and sidestepped in front of him.

Frustrated, helpless, he dropped to his knees and threw his arms around her legs. "Let me die, Morrigunia. Please let me die! I can not live with the guilt of knowing what I have helped set into motion!"

Pity flittered through the Goddess' heart and she threaded her fingers through his damp curls and held his head to her belly. He was shuddering with grief, his body trembling against her. He was racked with sobs that came from the very marrow of his being.

"Hush now, Beloved," she whispered. "I can not allow this." She put her palm against his forehead. "I will *not* allow this."

One moment the memory of seeing into the future was playing across Cainer Cree's mind and the next, he was unconscious, draped in the arms of the Goddess as she carried him to shore. She laid him down upon the soft sand and sat next to him, lifting his head and placing it in her lap.

"I can not allow you to suffer so, my sweet deargs dul," she said as she smoothed her palm over his forehead several times, wiping away the violent memory and replacing it with tranquility.

Long into the twilight, she sat there holding him, staring out at the brilliant red sun as it sank beneath the horizon. He slept on peacefully, unaware of the hands that roamed at will over his defenseless body. Neither did he feel the stony thrust of his root as it was worked to erection nor the impalement of the soft, warm cunt that enveloped him within its silky folds.

"Come for me, Beloved," the Goddess whispered, and felt the pulse of his seed spurting deep within her. She smiled, closing her eyes to the intense climax that shook her body soon after.

She had thrown the Geasa at him long, long ago but she was immune to her own restrictions. How many times, she wondered as she departed that lonely island upon which she kept the Reaper captive, had she taken him in such a manner? Just as he was unaware of her gentle rape, he was equally unaware of the sons he had given her over the years—sons he would never see nor even know existed.

"Nor will I allow your latest Reapers to get in the way of my plans," she said.

Chapter Fourteen

Queen Clea Robeus felt the blood rush to her face when she looked up to see Leksi Helios standing in her bedchamber. She put a hand to her chest as her head thudded forcefully in her chest.

"This isn't another hallucination," the queen said backing away. "You really are here and it was you who killed my father."

"You have nothing to fear from me, Your Majesty," the warrior was quick to say. He advanced into the room and went to one knee, his clenched fist pressed against his heart. "I am at your command."

Until this day she had never met the warrior, but she had an artist's rendering of him that she kept in a velvet-lined frame beneath her pillow each night. The rendering assured her of sweet dreams of the gallant warrior, and over the years that it had been in her possession, she had memorized the handsome man's every facial feature. As she stared at him now, she realized the rendering—as expertly as it had been painted—was but a pale reproduction of the man's true male beauty.

"Lord Leksi," Clea said in a breathless tone. "How did you...?"

"I would offer my condolences on the demise of your father but considering he was in the process of killing me when he met his fate, I would be lying. I am glad he is no longer among the living."

"As am I," she said with a dismissive wave of her hand. "But how came you to be here in the first place, milord? You say he was trying to kill you?"

"I knew you had no knowledge of what was transpiring earlier this day," Leksi said. "Lord Konan Krull and I were interned in your dungeon, and I was at the mercy of your father's torturers."

Shock washed across Clea's face and she got to her feet, her mouth dropping open. She snapped it shut and rushed to him, bending down to put her hands on his shoulders as she bid him rise, her eyes searching his face for signs of suffering. She reached up to cup his cheeks with trembling hands.

"You are all right? Did they...?"

"I am well, Highness," he assured her, and dared to take one of her hands in his and bring the palm to his lips. "Thank you for your concern."

"You are sure?" she asked, tears flooding her eyes. "You looked well enough in the dungeon when I saw you." She blushed. "I really did see you, didn't I?"

"Aye, Your Majesty, you did and I am fine." He smiled at her, and Clea's heart soared among the stars.

Flustered, she withdrew her hand from his light grasp and backed away from him, her palm tingling from his kiss as she laid it against her chest, crossing it with her other hand.

"I am here at the request of Lord Krull. He wishes for you to know he does not hold you accountable for your father's actions and is well pleased that you will sit the throne of Pleiades."

"Despite a veritable army camped at my door?" she asked.

"An army that came to rescue Lord Krull, Your Majesty," Leksi explained.

"They will not attack?"

"That was never their intention, lest Lord Krull had met his death at the hands of your father."

Clea reluctantly turned away from looking at that glorious male face, and walked to the window from which she could see the horses poised on the rise above the keep.

"Their intention is not to put me in chains?" she asked, her voice a tiny squeak.

"No, Your Majesty. The riders you see upon the hill are allies to you. They are all women save for Lord Krull."

She looked around at him. "Allies?" She shook her head. "Pleiades has no allies, Lord Leksi."

"It does now, milady," he told her, and came to stand beside her. He pointed to the left. "There are the Daughters of the Night led by Queen Mona herself. To the right are the Amazeens with Queen Deianeira in attendance. And those small bands of women warriors you see in the center are members of the Daughters of the Multitude under the leadership of Lady Galatea. They are all your allies."

"Such great women!" she said. "I have heard of them all!"

"With your permission, I will send my lady back to bid them come to meet with you," he said.

Clea frowned. "Your lady?"

Leksi turned and called, "Kynthia."

One of the most beautiful women Clea had ever seen walked gracefully into the room. Though she was clad as a warrioress, her femininity was apparent in the way she carried herself and the flawlessness of her tawny skin. The most striking part of her was the thick mane of silver hair that flowed to her waist. Clea's heart sank at the sight of this lovely woman for she knew without doubt this woman had claimed Leksi Helios' heart.

"May I present Lady Kynthia Ancaeus, niece of Lady Galatea?" Leksi inquired.

Kynthia came forward and curtseyed as gracefully as she walked. Her head was lowered with respect and did not lift until Clea bid her rise.

"It is a great honor to meet you, Your Highness," Kynthia said.

Clea's smile wavered as she held a hand out to Kynthia. "It is my pleasure to meet a Daughter of the Multitude for I have so longed to be a true member of that wondrous sect." Her smile returned. "It was you who made the mist, wasn't it?"

Kynthia took the older woman's hand and covered their joined hands with her other hand. "It was, and I am sure my aunt would be delighted to see to your initiation."

Despite the jealousy she felt to the very roots of her soul, Clea could not help but like the woman standing before her. There was no guile in Kynthia's expression, no malice or arrogance in her pretty gray eyes. She did not have the air of condescension about her that many of her father's guests had thrown at Clea over the years. Clea would have wagered that what she saw as she looked at Kynthia would always be what she would get—honesty, friendship and mutual love for the man standing between them.

Kynthia nodded. "I will always be your friend if you will allow it."

Clea drew in a long breath and released it. "That is good to know for I fear I could never compete with you, Kynthia." She smiled to show she was teasing.

"May I bid the queens come to meet with you?" Kynthia asked.

"By all means!" Clea said, clapping her hands. "We will throw the greatest feast in the history of Pleiades to welcome this new friendship between our countries."

Kynthia inclined her head, and with permission of the new Queen of Pleiades, left to bring Clea's new allies to the keep.

"You are a lucky man, Lord Leksi," Clea said. "She will make you a very good lady-wife."

"I believe so, too, Your Majesty," Leksi replied.

"Well, leave me now so I can dress for my guests," Clea said, then with a twinkle in her rheumy eyes told him he could stay if he didn't mind seeing her unclad.

Leksi grinned. "I could not swear I would not take advantage of you in such a condition, Your Majesty, and since Kynthia is a veritable harridan when it comes to my faithfulness to her, I would prefer leaving Pleiades with all my organs intact."

His words made Clea's womb leap with passion and she had to press her lips together to keep from groaning in frustration. Her palms itched to roam over his brawny body.

Reading her thoughts, Leksi departed as quickly as he decently could. He understood the effect he was having on her and made a mental note to try and find the lonely woman a suitable mate.

Or at least a randy suitor, came a giggle, weaving its way through his brain.

"Behave, Kynthia," he said with a chuckle, but was pleased to know he could hear her as he had heard Cainer Cree.

I'm better when I misbehave, warrior, she replied.

Leksi laughed out loud, surprising the guards he passed on his way out of the corridor that led to the Queen's chamber. He saw the men gaping at him, no doubt wondering how he had gotten past them in the first place. As they fumbled to pull their swords from the sheaths, he held up his hands—palms to the heavens—and simply vanished before their eyes, his Cheshire grin the last thing to disappear. In his place wafted a wispy fog that clung to the stone walls.

"Crimy!" one of the guards gasped. "Did you see that?"

"S-see what?" the other guard choked out.

They looked at one another, their faces pale and blanched. For a moment, neither spoke then the second guard shrugged.

"I didn't see n-nothing."

"Then me neither," the first guard stated. He lowered his sword back into its sheath. "Didn't see a goddamned thing what turned to fog!"

* * * * *

Despite having been told not to leave the Venturian capitol at Lyria, Kratos had ridden to Nebul for he had learned Krull and Leksi had been taken prisoner there. Intent on hacking his way into the keep if necessary, he had been pleasantly surprised to find the keep under the guard of beautiful warrior women. Taken straightaway to Lord Krull, afforded respect and admiration, Kratos could not keep from gawking at the imposing women sitting at the table with him.

"I think I've died and gone to my reward," the burly old warrior commented as he took a bite out of the duck leg he waved about to punctuate his words. "Lovely women to look at and food so tempting I can barely breathe!"

There was roasted pheasant and crisp, golden-brown duckling. Tureens of salmon poached in heavy cream and lobster tail dredged through drawn butter. Sliced veal and ham, and liver smothered in gravy. Pickled beets and corn on the cob, bright green peas and little red potatoes swimming in butter, crisp asparagus and freshly picked tomatoes right off the vine filled bowl after bowl on the banquet table. Wines flowed and ale sparkled in crystal goblets. Milk and ice-cold lemonade vied with rich Rysalian coffees and Chrystallusian teas to please the palates of the feast-goers. Crisp breads and pudding breads, soft rolls and fried cakes were used to sop up the various gravies and sauces. The dessert trays were laden with pies of every fruit and rich cakes piled high with layer upon layer spread with luscious frostings.

There was also laughter and jokes flying like butterflies through the long room that had not been used for such a joyous occasion since long before Abalam Robeus had taken the throne of Pleiades. Smiles abounded and teasing was the order of the day as three sects of women sat together for the first time without the rivalry that had always been present at such gatherings.

Outnumbered ten to one, Leksi, Kratos, and Konan Krull were amazed at the bawdy comments bandying about and aimed at the attractive male servants who carried in the platters and trenchers of food.

"Look at that ass, would you?" a woman said loudly. "I'd love to get my hands on that!"

"I'd rather wrap my fingers around his cock!" another guffawed. "Come here, baby, and let me see if you'd fit in my cunt!"

Konan's face turned dull red beneath the onslaught of off-color comments and he had to cover his shock behind the crisp linen of his napkin.

Kratos grinned as he chewed a large mouthful of succulent ham.

Leksi lowered his head and hid his eyes beneath the canopy of his hand.

"Ladies," Clea said, laughing. "Let's keep it clean while our three male guests are in attendance. We are upsetting their sense of propriety."

Queen Deianeira raised her glass of Chalean brandy. "Here's to the embarrassment of men. May it always be there to amuse us!"

"Here! Here!" rang out around the table.

Clea leaned over to speak to the Lord High Commander who—because of his high rank—was seated to her right.

"Pay no attention to them, Commander. Drink does strange things to us all," she apologized.

Konan looked up from his plate and found Queen Mona staring at him, her eyes hot with lust and he looked quickly away. He could not be in the same room with the woman and not want to strangle her for what she had done long ago, yet he found he had pity for her left within him.

"No need to concern yourself, Your Highness," Konan replied. "We men should retire and leave you ladies to your merriment."

Kynthia was holding Leksi's hand, and when she heard those words, slipped her fingers from his grip. She looked at him and smiled. "Be gone with you, warrior, else you might find yourself on your back, being wedged by every hot sheath in here."

Leksi took up his goblet and drained the last of his Chrystallusian plum wine. He pushed his chair back, stood then bent over to place a light kiss on Kynthia's cheek. But before his mouth could touch her face, she turned so that their mouths locked and she kissed him long and hard, to the hoots of the women around them. When she released her hold on his lips, she winked at him.

"Now they know who they'll have to fight if they want a taste of those luscious lips, warrior," she said.

Leksi blushed to the tips of his toes and backed away from the table, bumping into Kratos who reached out to steady his captain.

"Ever stray from that pretty wife of yours, Lord Krull?" a Hell Hag called out.

Konan shook his head. "No, Lady. I..."

"He did once," Queen Mona said. "And it nearly destroyed him."

Their eyes met and Konan could feel the chill of those words, but he could also sense the sorrow in them.

"Go to your lonely bed, Koni," Mona said. "Have faith that not a single one of us will slip between your sheets or your strong, hairy thighs." She looked away from him.

"But you'd best lock your door just in case, pretty one!" Queen Deianeira said with a hoot.

"Get your sheets warm for me, warrior," Kynthia called out, making sure every woman there knew she had claimed Leksi Helios. "I'll be along shortly."

A chorus of boos rang out, but it was a good-natured caterwauling. No woman there wanted to fight a Daughter of the Multitude—especially one who was no longer completely human—for the man she had branded her own.

With the men gone from the table, the women settled down and it was Lady Galatea who brought their attention to her.

"We all know," she began, "there will always be war. The Venturians will fight the Rysalians and the Rysalians will fight the Ordonese. The Qabalans will sit with their thumbs up their collective asses and watch while the world destroys itself around them."

"Which leads us to this," Queen Deianeira spoke up. "We have decided to annex Qabala and make it a part of Pleiades."

Clea winced. "I'm not sure I wish to rule such a people as the Qabalans. They are so…so…" She shrugged. "…useless."

"True," Galatea said, "but we would rather they be ours to command in war rather than standing there watching us be conquered by the Rysalians or Ordonese."

"What of the Venturians?" someone asked.

"We have nothing to worry about from the Venturians," Kynthia said. "They are staunch allies."

"True," her aunt agreed. "It is those Hasdu thieves in Ventura and Ordon that concern me."

"As long as I am Queen in Bandar," Mona said, "we have nothing to worry about with the Ordonese. Sekhem—for whatever his vile reason—has a care for his daughter."

"That *thing* is Lilit's father!" a woman asked with a gasp.

"Unfortunately so," Mona replied. "Believe me when I say I wish it were otherwise." She lifted her wine goblet. "I would have preferred she had been sired by Konan Krull."

Every woman there knew of what had transpired in Mona's room in Ventura. Though few approved of what she had done, not a one would condemn her for trying to garner a male child from the loins of such a powerful warrior.

"But what happens when you leave us, Mona?" Galatea asked. "Will Lilit pose a threat to the Daughterhoods?"

Mona squeezed her eyes shut and massaged them with the fingers of her right hand. "I don't know, Galatea. I wish I could tell you she won't, but I truly don't know." She lowered her hand, her shoulders slumping, and opened her eyes. "I hate to say it, but I do not trust my own child."

Kynthia settled back in her chair. She and Leksi had already discussed that loathsome child and had come to the conclusion that she would not be missed if she could be spirited away to a place from whence she could do no harm. Where that would be was anyone's guess.

"Perhaps you should send Lilit to Serenia," Galatea suggested.

Mona frowned. "To Serenia? Why there?"

"She is suggesting Lilit be sent to Galrath," Queen Deianeira answered quietly.

Every woman there knew of the infamous convent. It was a brutal nunnery, run by a group of sadistic nuns under the control of the Brotherhood of the Domination, a sect of priests considered to be the most evil of their kind.

Mona shook her head. "No, I can not do that. Not even Lilit deserves such a fate."

"Will you be able to control her once she reaches puberty?" Galatea inquired.

A look of fear passed over Mona's lovely features. "I don't know. I hope so but I..." She buried her face in her hands. "The gods help me but I don't know!"

"She is but a year or two away from being a woman," Queen Deianeira reminded Mona. "If she acquires her sire's powers, she will be a force with whom to reckon. Will you be able to meet that challenge, Mona?"

Despite the copious wine, and ale and brandy that had been consumed, the women gathered around the banquet table were now stone cold sober. Their eyes were locked upon Queen Mona, who was sobbing quietly, her shoulders heaving in her distress.

"No woman should be asked to remand her daughter into Galrath," Kynthia spoke up. "Perhaps we should relieve Queen Mona of such a terrible burden."

There were nods around the table and a soft muttering of "ayes".

"I say we cast a vote," Galatea suggested. "Those in favor of sending Lilit to Galrath, how say you?"

"Aye!" Out of the twenty women gathered, only one voice abstained from the vote but neither did that voice say "nay" when the vote was cast.

"So be it," Galatea declared. She looked to her niece. "Will you see to it, Kynni?"

Kynthia nodded. "Leksi and I will."

Sitting unseen in the corner of the banqueting room, Morrigunia shook her head. The women had made their decision, but it was not one the Goddess would accept. Disgusted, she quit the room and flew to Bandar, appearing before a stunned girl-child on the verge of her first monthly flow.

"Who are you?" the child demanded. Her pretty face was tight with an ugliness that spoke of her heritage.

"Never mind that. You had best be up, Little Sister," Morrigunia ordered. "They are coming to take you to Galrath."

Lilit jumped to her feet. "No!" she cried.

"Then call your lieutenants and have them fly you to Ordon," the Goddess directed.

"But…"

Morrigunia advanced on the child and grasped the slight chin in a stony grip. "Do you wish to be at the mercy of those hellish nuns?"

"No," Lilit whimpered.

"Then call your vampyre guardians, now!" Morrigunia released the child's chin and grimaced. The feel of that flesh disgusted her.

Lilit backed away from the tall red-haired woman and puckered her lips. A shrill whistle that hurt the Goddess' ears issued from the small mouth and almost instantly the whomp-whomp, whomp-whomp of wings could be heard in the distance.

In a brilliant flash of light, Morrigunia left the child. She flew unseen past the arriving bat-women and went straight to the Isle of Uaigneas.

Cainer Cree cursed when the Goddess appeared beside him.

"Do you like girl children, Beloved?" she asked.

He ignored her.

"I don't. I never have and I never will. They are willful little creatures that cause far more trouble than they are worth. Now boys are a dif—"

"Why don't you leave me alone, bitch?" the Reaper shouted. He covered his ears with his hands. "I can't take this!"

"Different," she finished. "Some, though, are just like their stubborn fathers. One such is Cairghrian. I have had more than my share of trouble from that lad although he will one day be a great warrior."

"I don't want to hear this!" the Reaper yelled.

"His father is—"

"Shut up!" he bellowed. "Just shut the fuck up, woman!"

Morrigunia watched the only human—well, half-human now that she considered it—she had ever loved run away from her. Once more, he was rushing pell-mell toward the heaving waves and she would have to intervene to keep him from trying to throw himself into the sea again.

Sighing, she thought little boys weren't the only ones who gave her more than her share of trouble. Sometimes it was their fathers.

Chapter Fifteen

Kynthia put her hands on her hips, dropped her head to her chest, and sighed deeply. "We're too late," she said.

Leksi went to the window and looked out. It was a sheer drop to the rocky slopes far below. "Surely she didn't climb out the window."

"No," Kynthia agreed. "Someone helped her escape."

"To Ordon?"

"To Ordon," Kynthia agreed. "Where else?"

Leksi pounded his fist on the ledge. "Well, that's a fine kettle of fish."

"Aye, it doesn't bode well for any of us," Kynthia declared.

"Do you think the Daughters of the Night will follow her when she returns?"

"More than likely. She will return a strong, determined woman, made even more determined by knowing her mother agreed to send her to Galrath."

"You think she knows?"

"I am sure of it, else she'd still be here, warrior," Kynthia told him.

"I'd like to find out who warned the little brat," the warrior seethed.

Kynthia closed her eyes and let her mind scan the keep but there were no flashes of insight that came to her. The minds into which she delved were free of the treachery. She slowly opened her eyes and looked over at her lover.

"Whoever informed the child of our intent is not at this keep. He or she must have fled with Lilit."

"I doubt it was a male," Leksi said.

"I do, too."

"Well, what now?"

"We go to Ordon," Kynthia replied.

Leksi arched his left eyebrow. "You think so, do you?"

"What choice do we have?"

The warrior shook his head. "Woman, you're going to get my head separated from my neck yet!"

* * * * *

Their horses had just cleared the little spit of land that bordered Ordon and Bandar when the sound of a mighty wind howling toward them caused Leksi and Kynthia to look back. Above them, the trees were suddenly being lashed with such a violent force the leaves were coming off the limbs in armfuls. Kynthia's hair blew free of its barrette and whipped about her head, stinging her face.

"Where the hell did that come from?" Leksi yelled. He blinked against the ferocious invasion of sand in his eyes and threw up an arm to ward off the flying debris tossed about by the wind.

It was Kynthia who first felt the unseen hand digging into her shoulder and she yelped, reaching up to try to dislodge the fierce hold. Unearthly fingers were wrapped over her shoulder and under her armpit and the pain of the grip brought tears to her eyes as she was jerked from her mount.

Leksi shouted as he saw Kynthia shooting upward through the air. He strained in the saddle, reaching for her dangling legs but she was flung out of his reach and the next thing he knew he was sagging beside her, his upper arm a band of fiery pain as they flew across the sky.

High above the treetops, skimming over mountains and valleys, and desert they flew. Rain lashed at them for a moment as they passed through a late evening thunderstorm but soon they were ascending higher into the clouds, chilled to the very marrow of their bones.

There was no outline, no silhouette and no hint of a being that had them in its grip. Hanging like someone's dirty wash, they were propelled along, flapping this way and that. Now and again, they would be thrust through low-flying clouds but soon they were so far above the earth with only the stars visible in the night sky.

"Kynthia?" Leksi called, urgently needing to make sure his lady was still alive and not the frozen stalk he, himself, felt like.

"I'm here, warrior," she said, though she could not see him as he flew along there behind her.

"What has hold of us?" he asked.

Before Kynthia could respond, they began dropping at such a rate she feared they would burn up like a meteor racing to earth. The jolt to her belly as she dropped made her want to throw up but she was afraid she'd drown in her own vomit. Glancing down and wishing she hadn't, the land was fast rushing up toward them and she closed her eyes, knowing the landing would be hell.

But the landing was as soft as a feather floating to earth and when Kynthia's feet touched the ground, the fierce pain on her arm disappeared. Falling to her knees, she landed with her arms outstretched and paused there on all fours, thanking whichever god had been listening to her silent prayers.

Leksi was standing still, unable to move, as rigid as steel as he slowly opened his eyes. He could see Kynthia on the ground and was relieved to see she was all right. His head was swimming, his stomach roiling as though he had been rolling downhill in a barrel. Other than that and the decreasing pain in his armpit, he felt well enough.

"Where are we?" Kynthia managed to ask.

"Welcome to Domhan na Gaoithe," an amused voice replied.

The warrior and his lady looked over their shoulders and found themselves staring at a beautiful woman who sat cross-legged in the middle of the air, hovering there like a placid hummingbird. She smiled benignly at them.

"That's Chalean for WindWorld," the woman informed them. "It's an isle similar to Uaigneas but to me, it is much lovelier. A little smaller but so much nicer."

"Morrigunia," Kynthia said between clenched teeth, and pushed herself to her feet. "You are Morrigunia!"

"My reputation precedes me!" the woman laughed. "I see my Beloved deargs dul has told you of me."

"Who is she?" Leksi asked, stepping protectively in front of Kynthia.

"You bitch!" Kynthia threw at her and made to go around Leksi. She had every intention of attacking the goddess, damn the outcome.

But Morrigunia floated up out of the warrioress' reach, tilting herself down a bit so she could see them. She laughed gaily as Kynthia jumped up and down trying to snare the goddess' foot to jerk her back down.

"It is a nice place as safe havens go," Morrigunia said, sweeping an arm in front of her. "There are fruit trees, vegetables galore, good drinking water and—I haven't forgotten the needs of my little ones—animals who will be accommodating with their blood and a grove of tener trees from which you can brew the drug you need to stay sane."

"This is a prison!" Kynthia accused. "Just like the prison upon which you cast poor Cainer!"

Morrigunia put a finger to her cheek. "Well, aye, it is, but a nice prison."

"But why?" Kynthia said, and was annoyed at the whine in her question.

"Because it suits me," the Goddess responded. "Be thankful I allowed the two of you to be together. I could have separated you, you know."

"Well, we'll just get the hell off this island and—" Leksi began but Kynthia groaned loud enough to wake the dead. He turned to look at her.

Kynthia slumped on the ground, her knees crooked, and buried her head in her hands. "We are stranded here, warrior. We can not cross running water."

"I can swim," Leksi protested.

"Try it, my sweet Reaper, and see what happens," Morrigunia laughed. "You'll find your parasite won't allow it."

"We crossed running water to get here," Leksi reasoned. "I remember seeing the Sea of Aziz as we flew over it."

Kynthia slowly raised her head and stared up at the Goddess who was once more hovering only a few feet above her. She looked into sparkling eyes that shifted colors from blue to green to violet to amber like oil floating on water.

"You have always had the power to take him off that island, haven't you?" Kynthia asked.

"He is where I want him and there he will stay for as long as it amuses me to keep him there," Morrigunia answered. "Just as you will remain here."

"But why?" Kynthia asked. "What did we do to anger you? What harm did we do you?"

"It wasn't what you did, child, but what you were about to do. You could not be allowed to interfere."

"Interfere in what?" Leksi demanded. He was kneeling beside Kynthia and had taken her into his arms.

"There is a war coming, sweet one," the Goddess replied. "You could not be allowed to try and stop it."

"How can you countenance that?" Leksi asked.

"Because she is the Goddess of Life, Death and War," Kynthia said, her shoulders sagging. Once more, she hung her head. "You can not have one without the other two."

"You will be safe here, Kynthia," Morrigunia said. "You have all you could ever need and your love with whom to share it. What more could you want? Ask and I will provide it."

Kynthia looked up. "The same thing Cainer Cree wants."

Morrigunia cocked her head in query.

"Freedom," Kynthia said. "We want our freedom."

The Goddess sighed. "Alas, that you can not have."

With that, Morrigunia faded like fog rolling away from water.

For a long while the lovers did not speak. She sat with her head buried in her arms, he sat beside her, his arm around her shoulders and surveyed their new home.

"It really is a lovely place," he said.

Kynthia nodded. "Aye, but it is still a prison."

"Only if we allow it to be," Leksi said. He got to his feet and held out his hand. "Let's see what the rest of it looks like."

Kynthia took his hand and allowed him to help her up. "Not right now. Just hold me, warrior."

He enfolded her in his arms, cradling her head against his powerful chest.

"You think we should make the most of this place," she accused.

"I think we should start a dynasty right here," Leksi said.

"Of Reapers," Kynthia said. She looked up at him. "You know I can only conceive male children. Remember I told you?"

"No, but what's wrong with that?"

"An island full of males with no females to ease their loneliness. Is that what you would like to see happen?"

A frown marred the warrior's handsome face as he thought about that. For years, he had searched for the right woman and during all that time, he had known loneliness even with hundreds of females right under his nose.

"Do you want that for our sons?" she pressed.

"Hell, no," Leksi snapped then yelled Morrigunia's name at the top of his lungs.

"I'm never that far away that you need to shout, child," the Goddess chided as she appeared sitting in the crook of an oak tree.

"What about our sons? Will there be girls for them?"

A tender smile stretched the lovely deity's mouth. "One for each of them, I would imagine."

"And girls for the sons of those sons?"

"For as long as it amuses me to keep you here," was the reply.

Kynthia drew in a breath. "Does that mean it won't be forever?" she asked, her heart thudding hard in her chest.

The Goddess shrugged. "Who knows, child? Perhaps one day I'll even remove my beloved deargs dul from his tropical prison."

"But when..." Kynthia began, but once more the fickle Goddess faded from view.

"It may not be as bad as you imagine, Kynni," Leksi told her.

Kynthia sighed. "Perhaps you're right." She settled into his arms again and when he chuckled looked up at him. "What?"

"I just realized I'm right back where I started," he laughed.

"How do you mean?"

"The prisoner of a powerful woman," he explained. "First your aunt and now your goddess."

"She's not *my* goddess," Kynthia disagreed. "I know of her only what Cainer told me." She swatted him lightly on the chest. "Besides, you are more my prisoner than hers."

"You think so?" he asked.

"And I intend to make you earn your keep here, warrior."

He turned her so that she was anchored close to his hip and began walking with her. The waves were gently lapping the shoreline and overhead the gulls were careening on the thermals.

"I don't know where this place is but when we left Bandar, it was full night. Now, I'd say it is midmorning, wouldn't you?"

"Aye," Kynthia agreed.

"We're a long way from home, my love."

"Tell me it will be all right, warrior," she asked. "Please tell me we won't know the loneliness Cainer feels."

"We have something Cainer does not have, milady," he said softly. "We have each other."

They stopped at the edge of the shoreline and watched as dolphins arched through the water in near the beach. Overhead, the gulls called to them and sailed gracefully by, seeming to eye the couple. In the distance, they heard a rumble of thunder and saw a fork of lightning lace across the sky.

"We'd best look for shelter," Leksi advised.

"She would have thought of that," Kynthia told him. "There will be a hut waiting for us."

"Then let's go find our bed for I feel a nap coming on," her warrior said with a pretend yawn.

"Liar," she teased, rubbing her elbow against his ribs. "You're more apt to have other things in mind for that bed than a nap."

"You wouldn't have it any other way, wench," Leksi assured her.

She gazed into his sensual amber eyes and smiled. "You're right, warrior. I wouldn't."

"But I don't really need a bed for what I have in mind right now," Leksi said, his words a soft growl.

Kynthia cocked a brow. "And what, pray tell, do you have in mind?"

One moment they were standing on the soft sand and the next Kynthia was lying beneath her lover, his body pressed heavily atop her own and wedged between her spread thighs.

"Not bad," she said. "I didn't even see you move."

"This deargs dul stuff is really sweet," Leksi stated. He lowered his head to nuzzle her neck. "I think I'm going to enjoy these powers."

"Well, don't let them go to your head," Kynthia said in a dry tone.

"Which head?" he countered, his tongue lapping along the column of her throat.

Kynthia smiled and put a hand to his hair, spearing her fingers through the dark mass and enjoying the silky feel of it against her skin.

"You know we could—" she began, but he cut her off with a low shush.

His sword hand was on her breast, kneading the lush globe through the fabric of her shirt, his thumb stroking over the sensitive peak with each light squeeze. Hungry mouth suckling at the base of her throat, he swirled his tongue in the suprasternal notch, tasting her flesh, drawing upon her.

Kynthia sighed deep in her throat as he plucked at her nipple. The sensation of his nails lightly pinching her erect nub sent shivers racing along her spine. She continued threading her fingers through his hair, gently scratching his scalp.

Leksi shifted down her willing body until he could push himself up, sitting on his heels as he leaned down and ripped open her shirt. "She'll have thought of clothing, right?" he asked.

Kynthia shrugged. "Who needs clothing in paradise, warrior?"

"Who indeed?' he quipped, laying aside the torn panels of her shirt to reveal her bosom to his view. He stared at those lush globes for a long while then slowly undid his shirt, flicking aside the buttons then peeling the garment from him.

Kynthia smiled as he stood up to remove his britches. His erection proved to be a bit of a hindrance to taking them off but when it sprang into view, her eyes widened and she flicked out a tongue to wet her lips.

"Tease," he named her as he kicked the britches aside and dropped down beside her once more, hard and naked to her view.

With infinite care he put his hands on those ripe orbs and worshipped them with loving grips that went from her chest to the straining peaks and back again, fingers closing over the nipples to lightly pull and work the coral flesh.

Closing her eyes to the pleasure, Kynthia felt his fingers trailing along her sides, spanning her waist then moving upward to stroke her rib cage. He brushed the backs of his fingers along her armpit then spiraled them down to her hip.

"So beautiful," he whispered. He shifted his body until his long legs were stretched out, his toes digging into the warm sand.

Releasing her hold on his hair as Leksi moved further down her body, Kynthia lifted her arms above her head and crooked one over her eyes to blot out the blazing sun overhead.

Pressing his palm against the flat indention of her belly, he just grazed the deep indention of her belly button, his middle finger tapping at that sensitive abyss.

Kynthia raised her knees and hooked them over his shoulders, giving him permission to delve into the hot, moist area that ached for his touch.

The warrior slid his hand over her pubic mound until the heel of his palm was pressed hard against her opening. He dropped light kisses upon her abdomen, flicking his tongue out like a serpent to taste her flesh. Laying his head against her thigh, he reached up to stroke the heat of her vagina.

"Umm," Kynthia agreed with a deep sigh. Her ankles were crossed over his back, the heel of her right foot resting against his spine. She smiled as he found the swollen bud of her clit and gently rolled it between his fingers.

Leksi could smell her heat and the moistness that was beginning to ooze from her core. The scent drove him mad with desire, and it was all he could do not to fling himself upon her and ram his hard cock into her as far as it would go. The sensations rippling through his body were ten times stronger than they had been before being given the parasite and he suspected when his climax came, the experience would be mind-altering. As much as he ached to know that moment, he forced himself to go slow, to pleasure his lady first for he feared the lust gathering in his loins would overpower them both when he unleashed it.

It was an exquisite torment Leksi Helios practiced upon his lady. His fingers were warm and strong and his nails just long enough to elicit powerful sensations along her nerve endings. Her clit was straining, hard as a man's rod, and it throbbed with a fiery awareness that made her heart thud against her rib cage. When he pulled back the hood to tease that straining nubbin, Kynthia groaned, forcing herself not to push the warrior away.

"Will your taste be ten times as sweet, my love?" Leksi asked in a throaty tone as he lowered his mouth to her clit.

Kynthia had no way of knowing if her taste was any different to her lover now than it had been before but from the slurping sounds he made as he suckled her flesh, she thought perhaps she was giving him a treat he found irresistible for he was drawing upon her flesh as though he were starving. Squirming under his manipulations, she could barely keep from crying out. She had to bite her lower lip to keep from doing so.

Leksi found her taste far more intoxicating than before. Every nerve ending, every sensation was magnified many times over. He would later swear to Kratos that his cock was ten times harder than he could ever remember it being and that the smell of his lady was so overpowering, he wanted to cry with the sheer joy of it. His fingers were trembling as he gently slid them into her cunt.

Sucking in a breath as those strong digits thrust slowly into her warm cavern, Kynthia felt a ripple of passion grip her belly.

Her lover's touch was so sure, so steady, so deep as he impaled her upon his fingers, then turned them so he could search for that wondrous spot that made her groan when he found it.

"Here?" he asked as he pressed upward against that precious spot. "Is it here, my lady?"

"Aye," she breathed, and lifted her hips so he could have better access to that delicate indention deep within her vagina.

Leksi stroked her with the tip of his middle finger then lowered his mouth to her clit. The dual assault brought a hard shudder to Kynthia's captive body.

In and out he then slid his fingers, going a bit deeper with each passage. She was hot and slick around him, oozing with love juices that teased his nostrils and drove straight to the core of his manhood.

"Leksi!" she yelled suddenly. "I am going to Transition!"

He pulled his hand free of her flesh and scrambled to his knees as his lady began to morph before his eyes. The wiry strands of her lovely silvery pelt glistened as it sprang from her long limbs. He watched her twist over from the pain until she was lying on her side in a fetal position. There was nothing he could do to help her but tears filled his eyes as she began her transformation for he now knew the hatefulness of the pain, himself.

Kynthia kicked out as the muscles of her body contracted and expanded then grouped together again. Her bones popped, her sinews hummed and the tremendous heat being generated from her changing flesh sent her into a wriggling, twisting mass of tortured limbs.

Leksi got to his feet, trembling all over as he watched the woman he loved going through such agony. He put out a hand—wanting to touch her, wanting to help—but knew there was nothing to be done. Tears fell down his cheeks and as the salt of one crystal drop touched his lip, he felt the changing beginning in his own body.

Kynthia threw back her head and howled as the Transition settled completely upon her convulsing body. She scrambled to her feet and stood there in her wolf persona, shaking her thick mane from head to tail. She looked to her left and found her lover on all fours, his own transformation in the beginning stages.

Painful, aye, Leksi thought as his muscles elongated and contracted and his bones shifted beneath the skin. *Painful but exhilarating,* he thought, for the power was coursing through his veins and the strength enveloping his limbs. His nostrils flared, catching scent of his female, and he swung his shaggy head — half-man, half-wolf — toward her. His crimson eyes flared with lust and his leathery lips pulled back over wickedly sharp teeth.

Kynthia was pacing back and forth before her mate as he passed deeper into Transition. His scent was like nectar to a bee and she moved a bit closer to him with every pass. When he snaked out a paw toward her, she sidestepped away, tossing her head, teasing the male, not allowing him to scratch her. She padded a few feet away and sat down on her haunches, lifting a delicate paw to lick at the silvery fur.

Leksi growled deep in his throat, her scent embedding itself in his nostrils. The heat of her sex was a lure that drove him mad with wanting her. His Transition was almost complete and when the last wiry hair had sprang from his leathery skin and the last claw pushed from the end of his paw, he sprang after her, grinning from pointed ear to pointed ear.

Kynthia yelped and took off running, her long strides eating up the sand beneath her paws. Across the beach they sped and into the grove of trees beyond the shoreline. She knew he was fast gaining on her for he was — after all — male and much stronger than she. But she led him a merry chase through the forest beyond, putting trees and a large rock between them, a large rock.

She toyed with him for a good long while, keeping him at a distance. Her tail wagged playfully, enticing him, but when he sprang at her, her hindquarters dug into the sand and she raced away, her mate nipping at her heels.

When at last she was winded and the joy of the chase had began to wane, she stopped atop a sand dune, her sides heaving and watched him sidling closer, his tail down, his jaws open, dripping saliva. Though she feigned leaping away, she stayed where she was, her eyes locked on his intent gaze.

Leksi sidestepped toward her, gathering himself in case she decided to run away again. He knew he could easily overpower her and he was tired of playing and wanted to get down to the business of fucking her. Warily, he approached her, jumping when she jumped. His head was down, his tail between his legs as he neared her. He growled, she answered.

Kynthia sniffed at his muzzle as he rubbed his nose against hers and she licked that black leathery skin. She whined as his taste rocketed through her. He was sidling around her and when he stopped, craning his neck to sniff at her pubes, she lifted her tail out of his way, offering herself to him.

Leksi sniffed at the moistness under her thick tail and licked at the swollen flesh there. The taste rocked him and he growled, moving behind her with a speed that brooked no resistance. He reared up, locked his front paws around her waist and thrust his slick wolf cock into her waiting opening.

Kynthia lowered her head as his teeth nipped her neck. He was holding her in the position their animal kind had known for millions of years. She was totally his and subservient to the male domination of him. Her entire body trembled as he rammed into her and withdrew, rammed and withdrew again.

He was panting as he pistoned into his mate. Her smell was so strong, so powerful he was salivating, his teeth snagged into her thick coat and just breaking the skin. His hips moved back and forth, back and forth ramming his cock into her slickness, going deeper with each thrust.

Kynthia whimpered for the pleasure that was claiming her was so intense her legs threatened to buckle beneath her. Had he not been holding onto her hips to keep her erect, she would have lain down and curled up in a heap. As it was, her legs were trembling beneath his wild assault and every push into her sent waves of delicious warmth through her belly.

Leksi knew she was but a few moments from achieving the pleasure he wanted to make sure she received. His animal kin might not have cared if their mate was satisfied but that was not so with Leksi. There was enough human male left within him to care for his lady's pleasure.

The first ripple of release hit Kynthia with such force she whined. Her rear end was tight in Leksi's grip, his teeth snagged into her neck so there was no way for her to stretch out on her belly as her climax began. The sensation burst upon her in gripping waves that squeezed around her lover's cock in ever tightening clutches.

Leksi grunted as his cock felt those first hard squeezes along it. Her heat was tight around him, slick on his hard length, and when it rippled over him, he thrust harder, spraying his own seed deep within her wolf cunt.

Kynthia knew the exact moment he impregnated her. She could feel the seed wriggling up her body and searching out her womb. Great elation filled her heart and she whined. The hard squeezes of her climax slowly diminished so she could feel the last of his jerking deep within her.

Leksi held onto his mate's flanks as the last shudder of lust passed from him to her. His teeth were still in her fur but loosely now for they were both exhausted, spent, their panting loud. His back legs were trembling almost as hard as hers were and when she collapsed beneath him, he fell atop her, his great head lying close to hers.

She flicked out her tongue and lapped at his fur, enjoying the taste of him. She groomed him as they lay there, his muzzle on her left paw. When the last of her energy was spent, she laid her head on the sand and closed her eyes, his light snores making her smile.

When they awoke, the moon was out though the sun still lit the western sky. She was spooned behind him, an arm over his shoulder, a leg thrown possessively over his. Their naked bodies were glistening with a fine sheen of sweat as Leksi turned over to his back and gathered her into his arms, pulling her head to his shoulder.

"That," he said, "was an experience of a lifetime, wench."

"One we will repeat often, I think," she responded.

"Not every time," he denied.

"No," she agreed. "Not every time."

Leksi frowned. "You don't think that *will* happen every time, do you?"

She was silent for a moment then quietly asked if he'd like to see whether it would or not.

He did.

It didn't.

Nor did it happen the third time.

Or the fourth.

When they awoke again, the moon was fully out and the night air was washing sweetly over their naked flesh.

They stood, looked down at the place where they had claimed one another and smiled.

Hand-in-hand they headed inland as a soft breeze came in from the sea and the thunder rumbled closer to their little hidden island. As they walked, they spied the field of wheat from which they would be obliged to brew the tenerse that would keep their Transitioning on schedule. Around them were myriad animals from which they could draw the sanity-saving blood without harming the little creatures. And true to her word, Morrigunia had provided a patch of vegetables and more fruit trees than either of the lovers could name.

"It may be a prison but it is a silk-lined one," Leksi commented as they came into a clearing and found the hut that would be their home from now on.

"Books!" Kynthia called out. "We will need something to keep our minds occupied!"

"Quills and paper so we can start a journal!"

"Carving tools and fine wood so I can whittle!" Kynthia demanded.

"And a lyre so I can sing love songs to my lady!"

Kynthia looked at him. "You sing?" she asked, her eyebrows rose.

"Aye," he replied enthusiastically and began an old folk song he had learned as a child.

Kynthia stared at him, amazed at his lack of talent. "No lyre," she said beneath her breath. "Don't you dare give him a lyre!"

And in her heaven, Morrigunia laughed. Gently she delved into the lovers' minds to see what manner of book they would find interesting and conjured them to the island along with quills and paper, wood and carving tools, and a few other things the lovers had not asked for.

Then she found a lyre…

Enjoy this excerpt from

Longing's Levant

© Copyright Charlotte Boyett-Compo, 2004

"I rather like looking at you almost nude," Tamara giggled.

Evann-Sin glanced around at her then arched one dark brow. He held out his hand. "Will you come to me?"

Something in the warrior's voice touched Tamara and she did not hesitate. She placed her hand in his, allowing him to draw her into his embrace. With her face pressed against the coarse fabric of his robe, she snuggled against him.

"We need to think here a moment, wench," he said softly. "My feelings for you have been strong since the first moment I looked into your eyes. In my heart of hearts, I have claimed you as my own."

Tamara smiled. "As I have claimed you."

He frowned then looked away from her. "Can you accept me as your lover now?"

"Nothing," she stressed, "has changed between us. Am I cringing in disgust here in your arms?"

He smiled gently. "But will you accept me?"

"With all my being," she pledged.

He circled her tightly within his strong arms, his firm body pressed closely to hers. "Then, let's divest ourselves of any impediments."

The Akkadian lowered his hand to the cincture at her waist and tugged at the cord. It untied easily so he pushed aside the ties, the ends falling to either side of Tamara's trembling body. Slowly he eased his palm beneath the opening of the robe, smiling softly at his lady's quick intake of breath as his bare hands touched the top of her undergarment.

"Have you known a man before now, my sweet one?" he asked as he reached out to pull her down with him to her pallet.

Tamara felt a tremor of anticipation ripple through her lower belly at his words. "I am not a virgin, warrior," she replied.

Evann-Sin sensed the apprehension in her answer and shrugged lightly. "It matters not except I would prefer to know how firmly and deeply my sword can thrust before I would cause you pain."

A little groan of excitement pushed from Tamara's throat. His gentle voice—low and mesmerizing—made the hair at the nape of her neck stir and the buds of her nipples harden. The coolness of his hand through the muslin of her undergarment as his fingers grazed the tops of her breasts filled her with growing need.

"So soft," he said with a satisfied sigh, trailing his fingers from the top of one orb to the other, stroking her, soothing her.

When his strong sword hand dipped beneath the edge of her undergarment, Tamara tensed. Se drew in a breath as he pushed the material down to bare her breast. The firmness of his palm cupping her, weighing her, lightly squeezing, created heavy moisture at the juncture of her thighs and she groaned again, caught up in the heady anticipation of what was to come.

Releasing her, laughing huskily at her protest at being denied his touch, he divested her of her robe, made quick work of the undergarment then came to his knees on the pallet, ridding himself of his own coarse robe.

Seeing the wide chest thickly pelted with dark curls, the pectorals that looked hard as rock, the ripples of honed muscles stretched across his abdomen, Tamara sighed deeply. This man was not only pleasing of face to look upon, his body was a marvel of manhood—taut and powerful, sleek and defined, as a warrior's body should be. His arms were sculpted with years of sword practice and—she had no doubt—weight training. His belly was flat, the navel sinking beneath a spiral of wiry curls that traveled downward to a commanding thrust from which she could not take her eyes.

"It has been awhile since my weapon has been sheathed in so lovely a scabbard," he said, drawing Tamara's gaze to his.

His words thrilled her and she reached for him, her arms aching to feel those broad shoulders, her body throbbing at the need to experience the weight of him atop her.

The Akkadian caught her hands, and pressed the palms together as though he bid her pray. He placed a feather-soft kiss on the fingertips then released his twin captives, stretching out to lie beside his lady, turning so his body touched hers from chest to toe.

"It has been awhile for me, as well," she told him.

Evann-Sin placed his lips to her ear and blew his breath lightly inside. Even as she quivered at the invasion, he used his tongue to lap at the sensitive inner surface, sending spirals of warm heat along the tender flesh. Another ripple of pleasure traveled through Tamara's tense body. "Turn over," he whispered.

She did not question his command nor hesitate. He moved back as she eased over to her stomach, her arms to either side of her head, gripping the pillow that held his scent.

"Spread your legs, my sweet."

Tamara opened her legs, reveling in the feel of him as he stretched out atop her. The demanding rigidity of his manhood pressed against the cleavage of her rump, sliding upward until it lay nestled along that fleshy valley.

"You smell of jasmine," he said huskily, and nipped at the sweep of her right shoulder, his teeth sending shivers throughout her lower body.

"Does that scent please you, warrior?" she asked breathlessly, for his tongue had replaced his teeth in traversing the plane of her shoulder.

"It does, though gardenia is my favorite scent," he answered, shifting his weight so he could plant tender kisses down her spine. His manhood dragged down her leg, leaving a slight wetness behind as he pushed lower in the bed.

"Jasmine is an aphrodisiac," she said, and sucked in a quick breath as he nipped at her side, clutching the indention of her waist between his teeth.

"It is working," he said, and there was amusement in his tone.

Nothing could have prepared Tamara for the invasion of his moist tongue between her cheeks. She tensed, clenching the muscles of her rump together, but she soon found that was no guarantee of protection from his questing mouth for he used his fingertips to spread the cleft.

"Ah," Tamara sighed, as his tongue darted against the puckered […]. She dug her fingers into the pillow; dragging it around her face for the sensation the Akkadian was causing demanded loud and fervent moans of supreme pleasure.

"You like that?" he asked with a chuckle.

"Um," was her reply. She was quivering, her stomach muscles clenching and unclenching as her lover replaced his tongue with the insistent tip of a cool finger. Her breath coming faster, shallower, expectant, she groaned as that finger delved inside her.

Not deeply, not enough to cause even a suggestion of pain, the probe was gentle and possessive as it wiggled slowly within her.

"Warrior, please," she whispered, lifting her rump.

Evann-Sin did not answer her need. He gently removed his finger to trail his fingertips over her goose pimpled flesh. Trailing his nails down her thigh to the very sensitive surface of her inner knee, he smiled at the grunt that came from his lady's throat.

Why an electronic book?

We live in the Information Age—an exciting time in the history of human civilization in which technology rules supreme and continues to progress in leaps and bounds every minute of every hour of every day. For a multitude of reasons, more and more avid literary fans are opting to purchase e-books instead of paperbacks. The question to those not yet initiated to the world of electronic reading is simply: *why?*

1. *Price.* An electronic title at Ellora's Cave Publishing and Cerridwen Press runs anywhere from 40-75% less than the cover price of the <u>exact same title</u> in paperback format. Why? Cold mathematics. It is less expensive to publish an e-book than it is to publish a paperback, so the savings are passed along to the consumer.

2. *Space.* Running out of room to house your paperback books? That is one worry you will never have with electronic novels. For a low one-time cost, you can purchase a handheld computer designed specifically for e-reading purposes. Many e-readers are larger than the average handheld, giving you plenty of screen room. Better yet, hundreds of titles can be stored within your new library—a single microchip. (Please note that Ellora's Cave and Cerridwen Press does not endorse any specific brands. You can check our website at www.ellorascave.com or

www.cerridwenpress.com for customer recommendations we make available to new consumers.)

3. *Mobility.* Because your new library now consists of only a microchip, your entire cache of books can be taken with you wherever you go.

4. *Personal preferences are accounted for.* Are the words you are currently reading too small? Too large? Too...**ANNOYING**? Paperback books cannot be modified according to personal preferences, but e-books can.

5. *Instant gratification.* Is it the middle of the night and all the bookstores are closed? Are you tired of waiting days—sometimes weeks—for online and offline bookstores to ship the novels you bought? Ellora's Cave Publishing sells instantaneous downloads 24 hours a day, 7 days a week, 365 days a year. Our e-book delivery system is 100% automated, meaning your order is filled as soon as you pay for it.

Those are a few of the top reasons why electronic novels are displacing paperbacks for many an avid reader. As always, Ellora's Cave and Cerridwen Press welcomes your questions and comments. We invite you to email us at service@ellorascave.com, service@cerridwenpress.com or write to us directly at: 1056 Home Ave. Akron OH 44310-3502.

erridwen, the Celtic Goddess of wisdom, was the muse who brought inspiration to storytellers and those in the creative arts. Cerridwen Press encompasses the best and most innovative stories in all genres of today's fiction. Visit our site and discover the newest titles by talented authors who still get inspired - much like the ancient storytellers did, once upon a time.

CERRIDWEN PRESS

www.cerridwenpress.com